Friends for Keeps

My
Extra Best
WITHDRAWN Friend

Julie Bowe

 Dial Books for Young Readers

an imprint of Penguin Group (USA) Inc.

My extra-special thanks to
Kathy Dawson and Steven Chudney—editor, agent, and friends for keeps!

DIAL BOOKS FOR YOUNG READERS
A division of Penguin Young Readers Group
Published by The Penguin Group
Penguin Group (USA) Inc., 375 Hudson Street, New York, NY 10014, U.S.A.

Penguin Group (Canada), 90 Eglinton Avenue East, Suite 700, Toronto, Ontario, Canada M4P 2Y3 (a division of Pearson Penguin Canada Inc.) • Penguin Books Ltd, 80 Strand, London WC2R 0RL, England • Penguin Ireland, 25 St. Stephen's Green, Dublin 2, Ireland (a division of Penguin Books Ltd) • Penguin Group (Australia), 250 Camberwell Road, Camberwell, Victoria 3124, Australia (a division of Pearson Australia Group Pty Ltd) • Penguin Books India Pvt Ltd, 11 Community Centre, Panchsheel Park, New Delhi - 110 017, India • Penguin Group (NZ), 67 Apollo Drive, Rosedale, Auckland 0632, New Zealand (a division of Pearson New Zealand Ltd) • Penguin Books (South Africa) (Pty) Ltd, 24 Sturdee Avenue, Rosebank, Johannesburg 2196, South Africa • Penguin Books Ltd, Registered Offices: 80 Strand, London WC2R 0RL, England

Text set in ITC Esprit
Printed in the U.S.A.
1 3 5 7 9 10 8 6 4 2

Library of Congress Cataloging-in-Publication Data
Bowe, Julie, date.
My extra best friend / Julie Bowe.
p. cm.   (Friends for keeps)
Summary: Ida May is surprised and angry when Elizabeth, her old best friend who moved away and did not answer any of her letters, shows up at summer camp with a new look and hopes of reestablishing their former relationship.
ISBN 978-0-8037-3692-4 (hardcover)
[1. Best friends—Fiction. 2. Friendship—Fiction. 3. Camps—Fiction. 4. Interpersonal relations—Fiction.] I. Title.
PZ7.B671943Mwe 2010   [Fic]—dc23   2011035685

Books in the
Friends for Keeps series
by Julie Bowe

WITHDRAWN

They say you can't judge a book
by its cover. But it doesn't hurt to
have a wonderful artist illustrating it.
This book, cover and all,
is for Jana Christy.

My
Extra Best
Friend

Chapter 1

I'm Ida May and I could use a little light. That's because I'm digging around in my bedroom closet, trying to find my flashlight. If I *had* a flashlight, it would make looking for one a lot easier. The lightbulb on my closet ceiling burnt out last week. I'm too short to change it, even if I stand on my desk chair. Even if I stack ten chapter books on it first. The books make me tall enough, but then I'm too chicken to let go of the chair and reach up to the ceiling. I'm better at reading books than wobbling on them.

My BFF, Stacey Merriweather, is tall enough to reach the ceiling with just a chair and her tiptoes. I know because we play in here a lot. We both have VBIs. Very Big Imaginations. Which means we're good at changing small, messy spaces into something else. Rabbit holes. Spaceships. Castle towers.

Jenna Drews, my other BFF, has a big imagination too, but her closet is a lot neater than mine. She even hangs her clothes in the order of a rainbow. Red. Orange. Yellow. Blue. Purple.

I hang mine in the order of a bag of M&M'S. *If* I remember to hang them up at all. It's summer vacation, so I'm too busy going to the pool and eating slushies and having sleepovers with Stacey and Jenna to remember little things like finding hangers and making my bed and cleaning my fish tank.

I better do that last one soon, though, or my goldfish, Pic, will probably pack up his food flakes and plastic seaweed and favorite marble and move to a cleaner tank while I'm at camp.

That's why I'm looking for a flashlight. It's on the *What to Bring to Camp* list that came with a letter from Camp Meadowlark. Flashlight. Sleeping bag. Bug spray. Swimsuit. There's also a list of stuff *not* to bring. Cell phones. Fireworks. Candy.

It's Saturday, and we leave for camp tomorrow and stay there for a whole week. Me, Jenna,

Stacey, Randi, Brooke, Meeka, and Jolene. All my friends from fourth grade.

At first when we decided to go, I had hummingbirds in my stomach because I've never been away from home for more than a sleepover. But then Jenna told me about all the fun stuff we'll do. Swimming. Hiking. Crafts. She's been to camp before. And Stacey assured me that living someplace else for a little while isn't so bad. She moves a lot because her mom lives here in Purdee, Wisconsin, and her dad lives somewhere else.

As long as I get to be with Jenna and Stacey, I don't care where I live.

I shift stuff in my closet, tossing aside old dress-up shoes and dolls, until I find my flashlight. I knew it was in here because Stacey and I used it the last time we played runway models. It's Stacey's favorite game. I like treasure hunters better, but when you have a best friend, you don't always get to choose.

Pressing the button on the flashlight, I make its bright beam skip around until it lands on my fairy princess sleeping bag. "You're on my list too," I say to the fairy princess.

She smiles up at me. When I was little, I liked to crawl inside and hop over to my mirror so I could see what I would look like if I had royal blood. Sometimes I'd even duck my head inside and imagine myself wearing her gold crown and permanent smile.

But I don't do that anymore. I can borrow a real crown anytime I want because Brooke Morgan has tons from all the pageants she's been in. And now that I have *two* BFFs, I've got my own permanent smile.

The bright beam flickers.

I give the flashlight a jiggle.

The beam blips out and everything is dark again.

"Batteries," I say. "One more thing I need for camp."

I pick up my sleeping bag and step out of the closet. Something else comes with it. An old brown blanket with a shaggy yarn tail.

Right away I know what it is. Half of the horse costume that my last best friend, Elizabeth, and I wore for our Halloween party in third grade. She was the front end of the horse. I was the butt end.

That was when Brooke and Jenna started calling her Eliza*butt*. Because they mixed us up and thought she was in back. People mixed us up a lot back then because we looked the same and were always together.

Then Brooke and Jenna started calling me I-*duh* because they thought it was dumb to dress up like a horse in the first place.

I think name calling is way dumber.

But that was a long time ago. Before I started being friends with Jenna and sometimes Brooke.

"I wonder if Elizabeth still has her half," I say to my sock monkey, George, as I pull the costume loose from the sleeping bag. He's supervising from my bed. "Probably not. She left everything behind when she moved from Wisconsin to New Mexico, including me."

I fiddle with the horse's tail. "Not one letter from her, George. Not even a postcard. Even though she said she didn't want to move to a place with cactus instead of trees. *Yucca*. She didn't want to wear leather fringe and ride a horse to school. Plus, she knew her teacher would make her learn how to spell *Albuquerque*. Maybe even how to rope cattle. Elizabeth didn't want to learn how to do any of those things, but I guess she changed her mind."

I drop the costume and rub my stomach. Not because of the hummingbirds. Because of the sore spot that starts to ache every time I forget not to think about her.

There's a knock on my bedroom door.

Jenna's head pokes in.

Stacey's too.

And Brooke's.

"Ready?" Jenna says, stepping inside. She's dressed in her red one-piece and orange flip-flops. A yellow beach towel hugs her neck.

"Oops," I say, tossing the sleeping bag and horse costume aside. "I forgot we were going to the pool. I've been packing for camp."

"Do it later," Brooke says, slipping past Jenna and hopping onto my bed. "If we don't beat the boys, they'll steal the sunniest spot. *I* need to work on my tan before we leave for Camp Prairie-lark."

"*Meadow*lark," Jenna corrects her. "And tanning is totally unhealthy." She checks her watch.

"Still, if we don't get to the pool soon, the boys will *rule* the place."

"*Girls* rule," Stacey says. "Boys *drool*!"

We giggle.

"The point *is*," Brooke butts in, "packing can wait. *I* can't." She melts back on my bed like a drama queen. Right on top of George. "Ew," she says, making a face and pulling him out from under her. "This thing stinks."

George narrows his black button eyes.

Brooke dangles him by his skinny tail. "What's it made out of? Gym socks?" She tosses George aside. He grunts when he hits the floor.

"Be nice to George," Stacey says, picking him up. "Next to me, he's Ida's best friend."

"Next to *me* too," Jenna adds quickly.

"Exactly," Brooke says. "Who needs stuffed animals when you've got friends like us around?" She pulls out a pair of buggy sunglasses and stretches out again.

Stacey and Brooke are both wearing see-through cover-ups. They bought them when they got new swimsuits last week. Pink and purple. Two-piece.

When I mentioned to Mom that I would be a much better swimmer if *I* had a new two-piece swimsuit, instead of the one-piece I got at the start of the summer, she said I could fulfill my Olympic dream when I grew a size bigger. I even tried *begging* for the bright blue two-piece the mannequin was wearing at my favorite store, even though blue isn't my best color. Pink is. But begging didn't work. It never does. Trust me.

"Get changed, Ida," Jenna says impatiently, "or we won't get a good spot for our towels at the pool."

Stacey helps me hunt around for my swimsuit while Jenna quizzes Brooke with my *What to Bring to Camp* list. We all got the same one.

"Who cares about what to bring?" Brooke says when Jenna finishes. "I'm bringing everything I own. But the *Do Not Bring* list? L-A-M *lame*." Brooke may be a drama queen, but she isn't a spelling queen. "How am I supposed to survive a whole week without candy?"

"They have marshmallows," Jenna tells Brooke. "And chocolate chips in the trail mix. Sometimes we even get ice cream."

"I prefer frozen custard," Brooke snips. "And I only eat chocolate chips *if* they're not touching any raisins."

Jenna rolls her eyes.

"What I don't get is, why do we have a *boy* for a counselor?" Stacey says, tossing my swimsuit to me and taking the Camp Meadowlark letter from Jenna. She points to the first name on a list of everyone who will be living in our cabin— Chickadee. Alex, our counselor, all of us, and two other girls we don't know yet. Cee Cee and Liz.

"Alex can be a girl's name too," Brooke says. "That's what we call my cousin Alexis. She's in seventh grade and, trust me, she's *not* a boy." Brooke puffs up her chest and swings her shoulders.

We all giggle.

"Boys live at the other end of camp," Jenna tells us. "They can't come into our cabin and we can't go into theirs."

"Score," Brooke says. "Less chance of seeing Rusty and Joey. Did you hear? They'll be there too."

"And Tom," I add.

"And Quinn," Stacey says.

We trade secret smiles after she says his name because we both have matching crushes on him.

"What about the *extra* girls," Brooke says. "I mean, what kind of name is *Cee Cee*? Does she have a brother named Bee Bee? And a sister named Dee Dee?"

Stacey giggles. "Maybe their last name is *Alphabet*!"

Brooke sits forward. She loves soaking up an audience even more than soaking up the sun. "And *Liz* must be short for *Lizard*," she says. "I bet she sleeps under a *rock*! And eats *flies* for breakfast!"

Brooke laughs at her own funniness.

I dart to the bathroom with my swimsuit before I have to laugh along.

Chapter

2

We meet up with Randi, Meeka, and Jolene at the Purdee Town Park. It's the halfway point between all of our houses and Purdee Elementary.

"Let's take the shortcut, through the playground," Randi says as we pedal toward the pool.

"Yeah, let's!" Rachel, Jenna's little sister, chimes in. We picked her up at Jenna's house. "My legs feel like pasghetti."

Rachel's only going into first grade, so her legs are a lot shorter than ours, which means she has to pedal harder to keep up.

"*Spaghetti,*" Jenna corrects her. "And we can't cut through the playground. Remember? They're still working on the new swings and stuff."

I can see Bessie, the cow-shaped hedge that grows near the school wall. When Stacey first moved here, we hid secret notes behind her. We even made up secret names for each other. I know it sounds like a weird way to make a new best friend. But after Elizabeth moved to Albuquerque I was too sad to make one in the usual way.

We head around the school, ditch our bikes by the pool entrance, and hurry inside.

Randi takes off for the high dive. Rusty, Joey, Zane, and Dominic are already there.

Quinn and the Dylans are playing keep-away with a squishy ball.

Tom is treading water, probably trying to beat his record. Once, he lasted thirty minutes. Afterward, Quinn had to haul him home on his handlebars because Tom's legs were as wobbly as pasghetti.

Brooke kicks the boys' stuff out of a sunny spot and stretches out on her fuzzy purple towel. Stacey joins her. So do Meeka and Jolene.

"I'm going to play with Tess, okay, Jen?" Rachel says to Jenna. She pulls a diving ring and two squirty fish out of their beach bag.

"Let me watch you swim a little first. I want to make sure you are doing it right," Jenna replies.

Rachel slumps.

Jenna takes the diving ring and squirty fish from Rachel and puts them back in the bag. Then she grabs Rachel's hand and leads her toward the shallow end of the pool. "C'mon," she says.

"I saved a place for you, Ida!" Stacey calls to me. She pats an open spot between her towel and Meeka's.

I'm just about to join them when a squishy ball hits my leg.

"Hey, Ida!" Quinn waves to me from the water. "Get that, will ya?"

I toss it back to Quinn.

"Thanks!" Quinn says. Then he shoots me a smile.

Before I can shoot a smile back, one of the Dylans steals the ball and Quinn takes off after him.

"He likes you, you know."

I look down and see Tom looking up at me. He's treading water near the edge of the pool. His head isn't moving much, but I can see his arms and legs doing a blurry ballet under the blue-tinted water.

"Who likes me?" I ask him.

"Quinn," Tom replies.

I give Tom a skeptical look. Besides treading water and doing math problems in his head, there's something else that Tom is very good at. Teasing his friends.

"Yeah, right," I say, sitting down and dangling my feet in the water. "And Brooke Morgan likes mud wrestling."

Tom treads a little closer. "Remember that mini basketball you gave him at our holiday party last year?"

I nod. "Of course. I was his Secret Santa."

"I saw it under his bed when we were playing wizards and aliens yesterday," Tom continues.

"So?" I say. "That just proves he liked it. Who wouldn't? It burped when you bounced it."

"So-o," Tom says back. "Your name was written on it."

I twitch a little. Then I do a casual laugh. "That doesn't mean anything. Quinn's mom probably made him write that. So he'd remember who it was from."

"Uh-huh," Tom says. "And I suppose she *made* him draw a heart around it too?"

My eyes go wide, taking in this new information. No one, that I know of, has ever written my name on a burping basketball before. And no boy would ever *ever* draw a heart anywhere near a girl's name unless he meant business.

Tom snickers. "Better put on some sunscreen, Ida. Your face is starting to burn!"

I look away quickly, thinking this might be a good time to dive into the pool. *Did Tom tell Quinn he saw the heart? Did Quinn confess that he has a crush on me?* But before I can ask any questions, I see something red in the water and it's not my reflection. It's hair. Attached to a freckled head. Meaty pink back. Checkered trunks.

Tom dunks. Down, up. Down, up. Like a bobber on a fishing line.

Then he goes down for good.

A moment later, he splashes to the surface.

So does Rusty.

"*Dah*-dum . . . *dah*-dum . . . *dah*-dum . . . !" Rusty chants. "Shark attack!"

Tom grabs the edge of the pool, breathing hard. "Thanks a lot," he says to Rusty. "Five more minutes and I would have broken my record."

"I'm here to help, *Tom*-ahawk," Rusty replies,

giving Tom's head a friendly knuckle rub. Then he gives me the once-over. "My oh my, Ida, why so dry?" He slaps at the water, splashing me.

"Stop it!" I shove him away with my foot. I'm not usually a shover, but boys can be so annoying sometimes. Especially when their name is Rusty Smith.

"Sheesh, Ida." Rusty rubs his arm. "Easy on the merchandise. You break it, you buy it!"

I squint and shove him again. *Harder.*

Tweeeeet!

I look up at the lifeguard stand.

The lifeguard is looking down at me. She takes the whistle out of her mouth. "No horseplay," she says.

"Sorry," I mumble back.

"Hear that, Ida?" Rusty says, hoisting himself out of the pool. "Keep your hooves to yourself." He scoops up an armful of water, soaking me.

See what I mean? *So* annoying.

Rusty gallops to his towel. It's lying in a heap next to Brooke.

"Can't you *drip* somewhere else?" Brooke lifts her sunglasses and scowls at Rusty.

Rusty plants a soggy foot on her towel. "Us guys called dibs on *this* side of the pool the first day of summer vacation. If you don't want us dripping on you, then arrivederci someplace else."

He dries his chest.

Then his armpits.

Then his checkered butt.

Brooke's face goes sour. "Fine. Then *I* call dibs on the best side of the pool at Camp *Whatever*lark."

"Yeah," Stacey chimes in. "Us girls will *rule* that pool!"

Meeka and Jolene nod.

Rusty wipes his wrinkled feet. "There's no pool at Camp *Meadow*lark, you dorks. There's a lake. *Round* Lake. Good luck calling dibs on one side of a circle!"

Rusty laughs.

Brooke stiffens. She sits up and gives Rusty a very serious squint. "What do you mean there's no *pool*? Where do we swim?"

"I just told you," Rusty replies. "In the lake." He leans in. "You do know what a *lake* is, don'tcha? Smelly water . . . slimy weeds . . . mucky shore."

Brooke blinks.

Rusty grins. "Watch out for snapping turtles. They can take your baby toe in one bite." He clicks his teeth.

Brooke whips a look at the other girls. "Did you know about this?"

Stacey, Meeka, and Jolene shake their heads.

"Don't worry," Rusty says, patting Brooke's head like a puppy. "We'll protect you. Me, Joey, Quinn, and Tom. Your knights in shining armor."

Brooke squirms out from under Rusty's hand. "No you won't, *Crusty* Smith. We can take care of ourselves. Besides, Jenna told us the boys stay on one side of camp, the girls on the other."

"That's only for sleeping," Rusty says. "The rest of the time, we'll be your constant companions."

He honks his nose into the towel and lets it fall over Brooke like a blanket. "Nightie-night, campers!" Then he cannonballs into the water even though he just dried himself off.

Brooke marches over to Jenna, where she is helping Rachel in the shallow end of the pool. "Is it true?" she hollers. "We have to swim in a *lake*? With biting *turtles*?"

Jenna glances up. "The turtles stay where it's

shallow," she says back. "Just pass the swim test so you can go to the raft. Only fish out there, and they hardly ever bite."

I study my swimsuit.

Worm-pink straps.

Caterpillar-green swirls.

I'm fish bait.

I walk over to Jenna. "What if I flunk the test?"

"You won't," Jenna replies. "It's easy. Only tadpoles flunk."

"Tadpoles?"

Jenna slips her hands out from under Rachel. "That's what everyone calls the kids who have to stay in the shallow end. *Tadpoles.* Deep-water swimmers are called *sharks.*"

I look at Tom, who's followed me. He nods in agreement.

"Tadpoles . . . snapping turtles . . . sharks. Are there killer whales too?"

Tom snorts a laugh.

Jenna gives me a huff. "The only thing that's going to bite you is mosquitoes. Don't you trust me?"

I sigh. Nod. "Yes," I say. "I trust you."

"Good," Jenna says back. "Just stick with me and nothing bad will happen."

"Look at me, Ida!" Rachel sputters. "I'm doing the dead man's float!"

I look at Rachel.

Chin back.

Tummy up.

Arms flapping like baby bird wings.

Jenna rolls her eyes. "More like the *goofy girl's* float."

Tom laughs. "Good one, Jenna!" He smiles at her and swims off.

Jenna can't help but smile too. Sometimes smiles have a mind of their own. Especially when you have a teeny crush on a boy. She does. On Tom.

I hop into the water with Jenna.

A minute later, Tess pulls Rachel away.

Stacey jumps in behind me.

Then Randi.

And Meeka and Jolene.

Even Brooke.

We splash and squeal and dunk each other when the lifeguard isn't looking.

Seven goofy friends.

Chapter

3

"All packed?" Dad asks. It's Sunday. We're leaving today.

I stuff George down deep in my suitcase and tuck my sketchbook on top. "Uh-huh," I say, looking over the checklist from camp. "Clothes . . . flashlight . . . swimsuit . . . bug repellent—everything I'm supposed to bring to camp, plus some stuff I want to bring." I zip my suitcase shut.

Even though *sketchbook* wasn't on the list, I packed mine along. We'll have Quiet Time in our cabin every day to read or write letters. Reading is okay, but I'd rather draw than write. George wasn't on the list either, but I'm bringing him anyway. Brooke might think I'm too old for stuffed animals, but George would get lonely without me. I'll just keep him hidden.

"No candy though, right?" Dad says. "You don't want little critters stopping by your bunk for a snack."

I shake my head. "Candy is on the *Do Not Bring* list. I don't want to break a rule before I even get there." I decide not to mention to Dad that Brooke is sneaking a bunch of snacks along. Jenna had a fit when she told us. If Brooke gets caught, our whole cabin could get in trouble. But, secretly, I hope she's bringing Choco Chunks. They're my favorite.

"Good plan," Dad says. "Save the rule breaking for later in the week. Give the counselors a chance to drop their guard." He grins.

I make a face. I know Dad's joking. He used to be a camp counselor. All week he's been telling me about the things counselors *love*. Like how they *love* when campers short-sheet their bunks. Or sew their pants legs shut. Or hang their shoes from the top of the bell tower.

Mom pokes her head in from the hallway. She looks at Dad, then at me. "Is he being a bad influence again?"

I grab the handle on my suitcase and pull it off

my bed. It clunks to the floor like I packed it with bricks instead of clothes. "Like always," I reply.

Mom gives Dad a frown. But I can tell it's just a costume for a grin.

"Grab your pillow, Ida," Mom says, tossing my sleeping bag to Dad. "Then head out." She picks up my suitcase. "I'll catch up in a minute. It'll give Dad time to tell you how to booby-trap a cabin door."

Dad's eyes brighten. "I almost forgot!"

He tucks my sleeping bag under his arm and draws me into the crook of the other. "You'll need some rope, Ida . . . a bucket of water . . . and the help of a friend."

I grab my pillow and take one last look around.

Sunny walls.

Gurgling fish tank.

Cluttered desk.

I see the picture of Stacey and Jenna that's sitting on my dresser.

I smile, happy I'm bringing them along too.

Everyone is already at Jenna's house when we get there. All my friends, plus their parents. Mrs.

Drews is driving us to Camp Meadowlark. Don't ask me how the boys are getting there. Hitchhiking, maybe.

"Leave your things with Mr. Drews," Mrs. Drews tells us. "He will pack the van."

Mom and Dad add my suitcase and sleeping bag to the pile of stuff Mr. Drews is standing over. They chat with him for a minute and then start talking with the other parents. I wait to give Mr. Drews my pillow.

"Be careful with this one, Paul," Mrs. Morgan says, pulling a big pink suitcase up to Mr. Drews and parking it in front of me. "Brooke's pageant crown and sash are inside. We wouldn't want to damage the rhinestones!"

"Why does Brooke need her pageant stuff?" I ask.

Mrs. Morgan gives me a blank look. "For the talent show, of course. Camps always have them." She looks at Mr. Drews. "Don't they?"

"Sometimes," he replies, letting Brooke's suitcase *thunk* into the van's hatch.

Mrs. Morgan frowns at Mr. Drews, then turns to me again. "What are you talented at,

Ida? Singing? Acting? Dancing, like Brooke?"

I think for a moment. "I can draw."

Mrs. Morgan pauses like she's waiting for more information. "That's it?" she finally says. "What will you do? *Sketch* the audience?"

She laughs lightly.

I lift my shoulder. "If they hold still."

Mr. Drews chuckles.

Mrs. Morgan squeezes my arm. "Talk to Brooke, dear. She'll help you think of something you're good at."

I smile politely at Mrs. Morgan. And make a face when she walks away.

"Is she right?" I ask, turning to Mr. Drews. "We have to do a talent show at camp?"

Mr. Drews takes my pillow and squishes it into a corner. "It's just for parents at the end of the week. Silly skits, jokes. Everyone sings the Camp Meadowlark theme song." He leans in a little. "Most kids don't wear crowns."

I nod, relieved. I don't mind singing songs and doing silly skits as long as I'm with my friends.

Mr. Drews lifts my suitcase into the van.

Then he pulls his wallet from his back pocket and takes a photo from it. "I used to work at Camp Meadowlark," he says, handing the picture to me. "Almost twenty years ago now, but it hasn't changed much. Camper cabins. Dining hall. Crafts cottage. Ball field. That's pretty much it, except for the beach and lots of woods all around."

I study the faded picture. Two people standing by a lake. Round Lake, I bet. I squint, but I can't see any snapping turtles in the sand. "Is that you?" I ask, pointing to the man.

"Mmm-hmm," Mr. Drews says. "Minus the beard. And a few pounds." He chuckles again.

"Who's that?" I point to the other person in the picture, a girl holding a clipboard. "Jenna?"

Mr. Drews laughs. "No, Jenna wasn't born yet. That's Mrs. Drews. We both worked there."

"With her clipboard, she looks exactly like Jenna," I say. "Only taller."

Mr. Drews nods and tucks the picture back into his wallet. "There's no mistaking where Jenna's love of organization came from."

"Dad, aren't you done *yet*?" Jenna marches up

to us. "If we don't get going, those *other* girls will get the best bunks."

Jenna checks her watch and taps a pencil against the clipboard she's carrying. She's wearing a Camp Meadowlark T-shirt. The one she got last summer. Her hair is in two braids, like always. Bright red ladybug barrettes are clipped above them. The ones I bought for her.

Mr. Drews grins at Jenna. Then he looks at me. "Ready, Ida?"

I take a big breath. "For anything."

"Good-bye!" Rachel cries as we pile into the van a few minutes later. "Write to me, Jenna! Catch me a frog!"

"There're *frogs* at this place?" Brooke says, scooting in next to Stacey.

"Duh-huh," Jenna replies, buckling the seatbelt that's next to mine. "That's why they call it *nature* camp."

Brooke does a fake gasp. "*Nature* camp? I thought we were going to *nacho* camp. Obviously, I'm in the wrong van."

Everyone laughs.

"Too late," Mrs. Drews says, pulling away

from the curb. "Camp Meadowlark or bust!"

Meeka pulls a camera out of her hoodie pocket. She turns it on and looks at us through the screen.

"Say *cheese*!"

We squish together.

"Cheese!"

Click!

Chapter

4

"How much farther?" Brooke complains as we carry our stuff down a wooded path, past a row of little brown cabins. Sparrow. Bluebird. Hawk. Each cabin's name is painted on a sign above its front door. The boys' cabins have bird names too. We saw them on the way to the dining hall, where we registered. "My arms are stretching longer than my legs!"

Brooke stops to shift her sleeping bag and pillow, then starts pulling her big pink suitcase on its little wheels again.

"I told you to pack light," Jenna chirps.

Brooke grumbles. "I don't see why your mother couldn't stick around long enough to help me carry everything. *My* mom would have." Mrs. Drews left after we signed in.

"My mother doesn't believe in long good-byes," Jenna says. "Besides, I know where our cabin is. I know where *everything* is."

"Where's the bathroom?" Randi asks.

"Yeah," Stacey says. "I drank a gallon of soda on the way here."

"Me too," Meeka adds.

"And me," Jolene chimes in.

"There's a bathroom in our cabin," Jenna tells them.

"*One* bathroom?" Brooke's face sags almost as much as her backpack. "But there are *seven* of us."

"*Ten,*" I correct her. "Us, our counselor, and the other two. Cee Cee and Liz."

Randi sighs. "Ten girls, one bathroom. I hope someone packed diapers."

Everyone giggles.

Except Brooke.

"We're here," Jenna announces, stopping in front of Chickadee cabin. It's small and brown, like the other cabins we've walked past. A big pot of red flowers sits on the front step. *Welcome!* is written on it. A banner by the front door flutters in the breeze. A chubby bird with gray wings and

a black-and-white head is painted on it. A chickadee, I bet.

The screen door creaks open and a girl steps
out. She looks a little older than Brooke's sister,
Jade. She's wearing a Camp Meadowlark T-shirt
just like Jenna's, only her shirt has *Staff* printed on
it. Khaki shorts. Clunky sandals. Her hair is pulled
back in a frizzy ponytail.

"Welcome, Chickadees!" the girl sings, giving
each of us a warm smile. "I'm Alex, your counselor."

Jenna steps forward. "I'm Jenna," she says.
"That's Ida," she continues, glancing over her
shoulder, "and Randi, Meeka, Jolene, Brooke, and
Stacey." She looks at Alex again. "They're new.
I'm not."

Alex's smile fades a little. Then she turns it up
a notch. "Great!" she says. "An expert camper."

Jenna nods, then pulls out her clipboard. "I
made a shower schedule on the way here. It's
alphabetical. You're first."

Jenna holds the schedule up for Alex to see.

"That's very . . . helpful, Jenna," Alex replies.
"I'll look at it later. First, I want to meet the other
girls!"

Alex goes from girl to girl, practicing our names. She must be really smart, because it only takes her two tries to memorize us.

"Come on in and choose a bed," Alex says, holding open the cabin door. "Top. Bottom. Whatever you like. Just leave a bunk for Cee Cee and Liz. They should be here soon."

Brooke grabs the handle on her giant suitcase. "Excuse me," she says, barging past us and lugging her stuff up the steps. "I hear a top bunk calling my name."

When everyone is inside we stop and look around. A bed with a colorful quilt is just inside the doorway, in a little room separate from the rest of the cabin. Stuffed animals sit along it in a neat row. A desk stands next to the bed. Jars of pens and pencils. Pads of paper. Books. A laptop. Watercolor paintings are tacked to the wall above the desk. Trees. Flowers. Birds. One of the birds looks just like the chickadee on the banner outside. *Alex must be an artist, like me,* I say to myself.

"This is where Alex lives," Jenna announces.

"No kidding," Randi mumbles.

"The bathroom is through there." Jenna points to a door across from Alex's bed.

"First dibs!" Randi hollers.

"Second!" Jolene adds quickly.

"Third!"

"Fourth!"

I peek through a doorway into another, bigger room. It's bare except for five bunk beds—three on one side, two on the other. A window is on each of the side walls, and another screen door leads out the back. All I can see through it are trees.

"Home sweet home," Randi says, nabbing a top bunk, then heading into the bathroom. Stacey takes the next one over. Meeka and Jolene grab the bottom bunks underneath Randi and Stacey.

"Nine campers, ten beds? I'll take two." Brooke tosses her sleeping bag onto the top bunk that's closest to Stacey's, and parks her suitcase by the bed underneath it.

She looks around, frowning. "Where's my dresser? And my closet?"

"At home," Jenna replies, claiming a top bunk across the aisle from Brooke and the others.

Brooke grumbles, squirming off her fat backpack and letting it fall onto her bottom bunk.

Whump!

"If there's no closet, where am I supposed to hide my—" Brooke pauses, making sure Alex is still talking with the other girls as they wait to use the bathroom. "My . . . you know . . . my *stuff?*" She glances at her snack-filled backpack.

Jenna climbs onto her bunk and peers down at Brooke like a grumpy pirate in a crow's nest. "You were supposed to leave your *stuff* at home."

Brooke purses her lips and flicks back her ponytail. "I give you two days, Jenna Drews," she quips. "Then you'll be begging me for a share of the—"

Giggly laughter floats through the open window by Brooke's bunks. She darts to it, pulls back the colorful curtain, and gawks out.

"Ohmy*gosh*!" Brooke squeals. "Girls!"

Jenna rolls her eyes. "*Duh*-mazing," she sasses.

"There're six of them," Brooke continues. "Older than us. *Killer* cute swimsuits. One of them has gorgeously long hair. Seriously, she could star in her own TV show! I have *got* to meet her."

Alex looks over. "They must be our neighbors," she says. "Hawks."

"*Hawks?*" Jenna says. "Great." Only she doesn't say it in a great way.

"What's wrong with Hawks?" I ask, setting my pillow on the bunk that's under Jenna's.

"They have sharp beaks and talons," Jenna explains. "And I'm not talking about the birds."

"They look very friendly to *me*," Brooke says, pulling Stacey in for a look.

I start unrolling my sleeping bag.

Jenna watches me for a moment. "What are you doing? Take a top bunk. That one." She points to the empty bunk across from us. Then she leans in. "We can whisper after lights-out. Leave the bottom beds for Cee Cee and Liz."

I pull my suitcase onto my bed and unzip it. "I'm not used to sleeping so high up," I say. "George might—I mean *I* might—get altitude sickness."

"But how are we going to—"

Beep! Beep! Beep!

Jenna suddenly stops talking and pushes a button on her watch. She lifts her chin and zeros in on Alex. "It's time for our swim test," she announces, hopping down from her bunk and marching over to our counselor.

Alex looks at the watch she's wearing. "I was hoping the other girls would get here first," she says. "But it *is* getting late." She looks at Jenna. "You know the way to the beach, right? If you show the other girls, I can stop by the registration table and check on Cee Cee and Liz."

Jenna straightens up and gives Alex a very serious nod. Her hand twitches like it wants to salute. "Swimsuits *on*," she barks, turning to the rest of us. "We leave for the beach in *five minutes*!"

Randi clicks her heels and stands at attention. "Yessss, sir!" Then she yanks a swimsuit from her duffel bag.

"Quick, Stacey!" Brooke says, flying to her suitcase. "Get changed. I want to catch up with those Hawks!"

"Seriously?" Jolene says, stepping out of the bathroom as Randi ducks in to change. "You saw a hawk? They're amazing! Did you know some can see a mouse from a half mile away?"

"I'm not talking about the stupid birds," Brooke says, digging through her suitcase, grabbing her swimsuit, then ducking behind the beach towel Stacey is holding up like a curtain. "I'm talking about the Hawk girls. Sixth graders. Maybe even seventh!"

"Oh," Jolene says disappointedly. She loves animals like Brooke loves killer cute swimsuits.

Zip! Zip! Zip!

Everyone starts pulling out swimsuits and towels and flip-flops. Pink. Purple. Striped. Flowered.

I unzip my suitcase too, happy that I remembered to pack my one-piece on top even if it won't make me an Olympic swimmer.

But when I open my suitcase, I do a very surprised gasp.

Not because George has wiggled to the top, which he has.

Something else is on top too.

A new two-piece swimsuit!

Plus, a note.

> *A true-blue swimsuit for you, Ida!*
> *Have fun at camp!*
> *Love,*
> *Mom & Dad*

I pick up the suit. Blue top in one hand. Blue bottoms in the other. "It's the one I showed Mom at the mall," I whisper to George. "The one the mannequin was wearing. She bought it after all!"

I hug the suit, thinking this might be my best day ever. Even better than that time me, Jenna, and Stacey found six dollars on the sidewalk and split it three ways.

I close my suitcase and turn around. "I got a new suit!" I cry, waving it for everyone to see.

Stacey looks over. "Nice!"

"Let *me* see." Brooke peeks out from behind the beach towel curtain and studies my new suit like a math test. "Not bad," she finally says.

"Ooo . . . let me get a picture!" Meeka says, reaching for her camera.

I hold up the suit and do my best pose.

Click!

"Now one with Jolene . . ." Meeka says, shooing me next to her.

Click!

"And one with Jenna . . ."

Click! Click!

Randi comes out of the bathroom wearing a black one-piece and cutoffs. She dives in for the next shot.

Jenna's watch starts beeping again. "Two minute warning!" she tells us. Then she pulls off her shorts and top because she's already wearing her swimsuit underneath. Jenna likes to be prepared.

I hurry to the bathroom.

Close the door.

Take off my clothes.

Pull on the new suit.

Then I turn and study myself in the long mirror that's hanging behind the door.

Arms.

Legs.

Back.

Belly button.

I smile at my reflection. "You look killer cute," I say.

Someone pounds on the door. "Hurry, Ida!" Stacey calls out. "Jenna says it's time to go!"

I open the door, ditch my clothes, grab my beach towel, and head out with Stacey. We fly down the path like chickadees.

Giggling, like girls.

Hand in hand, like best friends.

Chapter
5

The beach is buzzing with campers and counselors when we get there a few minutes later. I
don't know how many, exactly, but it looks like
enough to fill a lunchroom. Some are goofing
around in the sand, but most are clumped along
a low stone wall that separates the grassy lawn
from the beach.

Rusty, Joey, Quinn, and Tom are there, with
an older boy. His hair is so red, it's orange. It flops
across his face. Orange stubble glints on his chin
like cookie sprinkles. He's wearing a staff T-shirt
like Alex's.

"*Dah*-dum . . . ! *Dah*-dum . . . ! *Dah*-dum . . . !"
Rusty chants as he and the other three race toward
us, raising their fists like champions. "We're real
sharks now!" Green bands dangle from their wrists.

They must have already passed their swim test.

"Was it hard?" I ask. "The swim test?"

"Nope," Quinn replies. "Easy cheesy. You'll do great!" He gives me a big smile.

Normally, I would give him a big smile back. Then I would give Stacey or Jenna a secret glance, because they both know I like him.

But that was before I found out he drew a heart around my name on his burping basketball. I don't know what I'm supposed to do when a boy likes me back. They never teach you that kind of stuff at school.

I glance away and pretend to be very interested in Joey Carpenter. He's crooking his arm like a shark fin and gnashing his teeth at Brooke.

Brooke swats him away. "Juvenile," she snips.

Tom does a sly grin. "That's *pup* to you."

Brooke squints at Tom. *"Pup?"*

Tom nods. "Young sharks. They're called *pups*." He tucks his hands under his chin and pants like a dog. The other boys join in, panting and howling at the bright blue sky.

Brooke gives them a snooty smirk. "I know a better name for *young sharks*."

"What?" Stacey asks.

Brooke sizes up the boys. *"Dumb dorks."* Then she turns away and scans the beach. "I'm only interested in *hawks* anyway. Do you see them? The girls, I mean. From Hawk cabin?"

"The place is crawling with girls," Joey says, dropping his paws. "Connor told us they outnumber guys two to one this week."

"Who's Connor?" Randi asks.

"Our counselor." Quinn points at the boy with the floppy orange hair. "He's awesome."

Rusty bobs his head. "We don't have to shower all week if we don't want to."

"*And* he's not gonna mommy us about changing our underwear either," Joey adds.

I wrinkle my nose.

All the girls do.

"That's totally unsanitary," Jenna says.

Rusty shrugs. "Keeps the girls away." Then he scratches his armpit and gives it a sniff.

"Not to mention the Meadowlark Monster," Tom adds. He does that sly grin again.

Meeka's eyes go wide. "Monster?"

Tom nods. "He lives in the woods."

"Eats campers for dessert," Joey adds. "The sweeter, the better. Connor told us."

Joey eyes up Brooke's bare shoulder.

Then he *licks* it.

Brooke howls and wipes away the lick germs. Then she practically shoves Joey off his feet.

"No worries, Brooke," Joey says. "You're not nearly sweet enough for *any* monster."

Jenna crosses her arms. "If there were a monster here, I would know about it."

Quinn shrugs. "Maybe he just moved to town."

"That makes sense," Tom chimes in. "*People* move all the time. Why not monsters?"

"Because monsters aren't *real*," Jenna says.

"Oh yeah?" Rusty replies. He turns toward their counselor. "Hey, Connor!" he shouts.

Connor looks up from talking with some other campers.

"The monster story's true, right?"

Connor grins. Gives Rusty a thumbs-up.

"See?" Rusty says, turning back to us. "Counselors don't lie. If Connor says the Meadowlark Monster is real, it must be true."

A lifeguard on the dock blows his whistle.

Campers trudge out of the water. Others tiptoe in.

Brooke suddenly gasps and points at some soggy girls. "That's *them*!" she squeals. "The Hawks!"

Brooke hops off the stone wall and hurries across the beach.

"C'mon," Jenna says to the rest of us. "If we don't take the test, they'll stick us with the *tad-poles.*"

I nudge in next to Stacey as we leave the boys behind. "Do you think there's really a monster here?" I whisper to her.

Stacey thinks this through. "Maybe. Maybe not. Sometimes older kids—even grown-ups—make stuff up."

I nod, thinking of the stories my dad has told me. Once, he convinced me and Elizabeth that there were fairies living under my porch. We'd leave them shiny beads and pretty pebbles. They'd leave us notes written in curly cursive. So tiny we had to use a magnifying glass to read them. Then, one day, we found one of the tiny notes on my dad's desk.

We didn't stop believing in fairies. We just stopped believing they lived under my porch.

"Maybe we should skip showering too, just to be safe." I give my armpit a little sniff.

"It wouldn't help," Stacey replies, doing a big, sparkly smile. "We'd still be too sweet!"

I nod. "Inside and out."

Brooke is talking with two of the Hawk girls when we catch up to her. One is short and curvy, with dark hair that curls like ribbon on a birthday present. The other girl is tall and stick-straight, from her long blond hair to her tan toes.

"It's totally easy," the short one says to Brooke as she dries off and pulls on a hoodie. "You'd have to be an idiot to fail." Something chirps in her pocket. She reaches in quickly and turns off a cell phone.

"You better silence that thing," the tall girl says, combing her wet hair with her skinny fingers. "I'm not sharing mine if they take yours away."

The short girl pushes a button on her phone and hides it again. She looks at us. "Pretend you didn't see that, kay-o?" She smiles like we're her new best friends. "I'm Nat, by the way."

"And *I* am Emillie," the tall girl announces. "Two *l*'s, no *y*."

Brooke's face goes all impressed. "I'm *Brooke*,"

she says. "Two *o*'s, no *c*. We should definitely hang out."

Emillie snickers. Then she gives the rest of us the once-over. "Which cabin are you *girls* in?" She says *girls* like it's spelled *b-a-b-i-e-s*.

"We're Chickadees!" Stacey replies.

Emillie does the snicker again. She and Nat exchange glances. "Thought so," they singsong together.

Nat slips a stretchy band off her wrist and pulls her damp curls into a stubby ponytail. "They always put the little kids in Chickadee."

Emillie nods in agreement. "How old are you *chicks* anyway?"

"Ten," Randi says.

Brooke gives Randi the elbow. "Almost *eleven*," she adds.

Emillie laughs lightly and reaches for a cover-up. "Practically out of training pants," I hear her mumble.

Nat wraps a towel around her waist and slips her sandy feet into a pair of flip-flops. "Catch you *chicks* later . . . kay-o?"

"Kay-o!" Brooke replies, waving excitedly as

Nat and Emillie walk away. She does a bright sigh. "Weren't they nice? So mature."

"Uh-huh," I say, watching as Nat and Emillie glance back, whispering and giggling. "*Real* nice. *Very* mature."

"I remember those two from last year," Jenna grumbles. "Don't get mixed up with them, Brooke. They're trouble."

"Don't be such a worrywart, Jenna," Brooke says, running her fingers through her ponytail.

Alex hurries up to us. "Good news, girls!" she says. "Liz is here! Her parents are getting her registered, then I'll take her to the cabin."

Jenna steps up. "But if she doesn't come right now, she'll miss the swim test."

"She doesn't want to take it," Alex replies. "Liz has already decided to stay in the shallow end."

"*Decided* to?" Jolene says. "You mean she *can* swim, but won't?"

Alex shrugs. "I guess."

"Huh," Randi says. "What kind of kid wants to be a tadpole when she could be a shark?"

"The kind with feathers," Brooke says, still running her fingers through her ponytail. "As in chick*en,* not chick*adee.*" She snickers just like Emillie did. Then strains to catch another glimpse of her and Nat.

"What about Cee Cee?" I ask. "Is she here too?"

Alex shakes her head. "Liz's parents told me she can't come. She broke her arm last week and may need surgery to fix it."

"Ouch," Meeka says.

"Bummer," Randi adds.

"Darn," Brooke chimes in. "Just when I was looking forward to meeting alphabet girl."

I frown. "So that means Liz came to camp without a friend?"

Alex gives me a nod. "She knew you'd be here, so she decided to give it a try."

I blink, surprised. "But she doesn't know me."

Alex shrugs again. "It seems like she does."

A whistle blows. "Your turn!" the lifeguard on the dock shouts to us.

Beach towels and cover-ups fall to the sand. Everyone takes off for the water. Alex heads back to the cabin. But I hesitate, thinking. *She must have me confused with someone else. I don't know any girl named Liz.*

The lifeguard blows his whistle again. He points at me. "Are you taking the test?"

Everyone turns, looking.

I drop my towel, kick off my flip-flops, and hurry across the sand. But it's deep, so I stumble. The next thing I know, I'm on all fours like a baboon with my blue bikini butt sticking up in the air.

"I see London!" Rusty shouts.

"I see France!" Joey chimes in.

"I see Ida's underpants!" they sing together.

The beach explodes with laughter.

Quickly, I take off for the lake again. The other girls are inching in, but I plow past them, not caring that it feels fives degrees warmer than ice.

All I care about right now is disappearing.

I plug my nose and dunk.

I stay under until my lungs burn. Until I'm sure all the laughing has stopped.

When I finally pop up, the other girls are at the rope that divides the shallow area from the deeper water. I swim-walk toward them as fast as I can, catching my breath the whole way.

"I want you to swim the length of the rope,"

the lifeguard on the dock tells us. "Do the crawl on the way down. Then back float here, to me."

Everyone starts in. I'm an okay crawler, but I'm still out of breath from dunking.

The boys are cheering and shouting out names from the shore, like we're racing. Only no one is shouting my name because I'm in last place. The more I try to catch up, the more I struggle with my stroke. Before long, the other girls are back floating toward me.

"Faster, Ida!" Jenna says as she glides past me. "You're getting left behind!"

I glance at the lifeguard.

He studies me for a moment. Then he makes a mark on his clipboard.

Calm down, I tell myself, crawling as fast as I can. *Everyone thinks the test is easy, so stop making it look so hard.*

I get to the end and start back floating toward the dock. But the faster I go, the more I bump into the rope, which is covered with slimy weeds. Plus, each time I take a stroke, my swimsuit top creeps a little closer to my chin. *What if it's around my neck when I get to the dock? What if everyone laughs again?*

I stop.

Flick a weed off my hand.

Tug my top down.

Glance at the lifeguard.

He frowns and makes another mark on his clipboard.

"Have a nice *trip*?" Brooke asks, shivering, when I finally finish.

I don't answer. My teeth are chattering too much. Partly because I'm cold. Partly because I know I'm flunking this test.

"Now I want you to swim out until you can't touch bottom," the lifeguard says. "When I say 'Go,' tread water for two minutes."

"You can do this," Jenna says as we duck under the rope and swim out a few feet. "Tom can tread water for *thirty* minutes. His arms and legs are way shorter and skinnier than yours."

"Go!" the lifeguard shouts.

I churn my arms and legs extra-hard.

I try to smile casually at the lifeguard, but when I do, lake water washes into my mouth.

I stop smiling.

The Purdee pool never chops like this. Plus,

you can see through pool water and keep track of the things that are skimming past your legs. Diving rings. Lost goggles. Other kids' feet. But you can't see through lake water. It's cloudy, like vegetable soup, without the peas and carrots. You can only imagine the stuff that's swimming around below you. Stuff with fins. And teeth.

I force my tired legs to do wild kicks, hoping I look too complicated to eat.

"One minute!" the lifeguard calls out.

One minute? It feels like one hour.

I sink up to my earlobes.

"Keep treading!" Jenna pants encouragingly. "Think . . . about things . . . you like!"

I concentrate on my favorite things. Sleepovers with Stacey. Bike rides with Jenna. Choco Chunks with George. Mom and Dad. My goldfish, Pic. Even Quinn.

But nothing helps.

My chin drops.

I sputter.

And start to go down.

My hands lunge for the rope. My whole body wraps around it, breathing hard.

The lifeguard looks at me. "You okay?" he shouts.

I nod. "No," I mumble.

I've never gotten an F on a test before.

But I know I'm getting one today.

My towel feels scratchy with sand as I wipe it across my face when we all get back to shore. At least tears blend in with lake water.

The boys have left, thank goodness. I see them heading toward their cabin, hanging on to Connor like monkeys in a tree.

I see Alex too. She's walking in the opposite direction, with a girl.

"That must be Liz," Stacey says, looking up. "Do you recognize her?"

I rub my eyes and squint. But I can only see bits of her from here.

Hair like mine, only boy short.

Glasses.

Mint-green hoodie.

Plaid shorts.

Bright red cowboy boots.

I shake my head. "I've never seen that girl before in my life."

Liz glances back just as the lifeguard walks up to me.

I hold out my wrist.

He wraps a plastic band around it.

Tadpole pink.

The other girls get wristbands too.

Shark green.

I look up again.

Liz is gone.

Chapter

6

"Cheer up," Stacey says to me on the way back to Chickadee. "I'll swim with you in the shallow end some of the time."

"I will too," Jenna adds, linking arms with me.

I do half a smile. I'm happy my friends aren't ditching me, but I still wish I wasn't a tadpole.

As we walk by the Hawk cabin, we hear loud talk and laughter. Brooke peers at the windows. "Do you think Nat and Emillie are in there?"

Jenna does a groan. "I told you to stay away from them."

Brooke gives her a squint. "You're not my mother, Jenna Drews. *You* can't choose my friends for me."

Jenna squints back. "I *am* your friend. That's why I'm telling you not to choose them. They're the kind of girls who *accidentally* squish your clay pot in crafts. And knock over your sandcastle on the beach. And yank down your swimsuit bottoms when you're climbing onto the raft." Jenna pauses, pinching up her swimsuit straps. "Why do you think I wore a one-piece this year? *Don't* trust *Rat* and *Enemmie*."

"Hi, girls!" Alex calls to us. She's standing in front of Chickadee talking with a very hairy man. His eyebrows look like woolly caterpillars. His beard almost touches his Camp Meadowlark staff shirt. And his ponytail is as long as Brooke's.

Jenna's eyes go all suspicious as we walk up to him and Alex. "Boys aren't allowed by the girls' cabins," she tells the man.

"They are if a toilet's plugged," the man replies, twirling a plunger.

"This is Pete," Alex explains. "Our summer maintenance guy. He's allowed to go in *all* the cabins." She leans toward us. "Be nice to him if you like toilet paper."

Pete grins and twirls his plunger again.

We give him our nicest smiles.

Alex points past our cabin. "Hang your towels on the clothesline around back. Then get dressed for supper. Liz is unpacking. Be *extra*-friendly, okay?"

We all nod and walk around back, rubbing sand off our feet and hanging up our towels to dry.

Liz is unrolling a sleeping bag on the bed that's closest to mine when we shuffle inside.

"Hi there," Brooke says, wiggling her fingers at Liz's back. "I'm Brooke. Two *o*'s, no *c*. Bummer about your no-show friend."

Stacey holds up a bouquet of dandelions. "We got you flowers."

"And a present," I add, cupping the rock me and Jenna found by the clothesline. Red, with white swirls. "It's an agate."

"Ooo . . ." Meeka says. "Let me take a picture!" She runs for her camera.

Liz turns around and takes the dandelions from Stacey. "Thanks!" she says, giving Stacey a friendly smile. Something about it looks familiar.

Then she turns to me. "Cool rock, Ida! It matches

my red boots." She giggles and does a little jig.

Jenna huffs. "Cowboy boots," she mumbles. "Totally impractical for camp."

I frown, studying Liz. Her voice is familiar too, but it doesn't match her face. Then, slowly, things start coming into focus—her stick-out ears, her freckles, the tiny scar on her chin. She lifts the dandelions to smell them and I see a faded blue friendship bracelet tied around her wrist. *The one I made for her in third grade.*

I squeeze the agate. "Elizabeth?" I whisper.

She gives me a smile that I've seen a thousand times before. "Surprise!"

"Oh. My. *Gosh.*" Brooke's eyes go wide. "I don't believe it. Eliza*butt* Evans. Since when do you wear glasses? And what did you do to your hair?"

Elizabeth's eyes flash to Brooke. "I'm *Liz* now," she says, clicking down her smile. "At least, that's what my friends call me."

Jenna moves closer to me. "What friends?" she asks.

Elizabeth gives Jenna a cool glance. Sniffs her dandelions. "Hello, Jenna," she says. "It's *soooo* good to see you again."

Jenna stiffens.

Stacey steps forward. "Hi, Liz," she says. "I'm Stacey. I don't think we've met."

"That's because Elizabeth . . . er . . . *Liz* moved away before you got to Purdee," Randi explains.

Jolene nods. "She was Ida's BFF."

"Since kindergarten," Meeka adds, turning on her camera.

Stacey's eyes brighten. "Oh!" she says. "*Elizabeth Evans!* I know about you. Ida told me."

"She did?" Elizabeth looks at me like this is good news. Like she thinks I told Stacey about all the fun stuff we used to do together. But, really, all I told Stacey was how she ditched me when she moved away.

I gulp some air. "Why are you *here*?" I ask. "Don't they have camps in Albuquerque?"

"Sure," Elizabeth replies. "But I still have family around Purdee. Aunt Sara and Uncle Tim. My cousins, Derrick and Cee Cee. Even my old dog, Champ! I was so sad when I had to leave him behind. But now, as soon as our new house is ready, I get him back!"

Jenna sniffs. "We're *soooo* happy for you."

I shake my head, feeling out of focus again. "You're moving to *another* new house?"

Elizabeth nods excitedly. "Not far from you! I bet we'll ride the same bus to school!"

My brain pounds against my ears. I must not have heard her right. "But that's silly," I reply. "We can't ride the same bus when you live in Albuquerque and I live here."

Elizabeth giggles again. "You don't get it. Daddy's boss changed his mind. He doesn't want us to live in Albuquerque anymore. *I'm moving back!*"

I squeeze the agate harder. "You're . . . moving . . . *back*?"

Elizabeth nods. "For good!"

Jenna huffs. "For *bad*."

"Squish together," Meeka says, waving everyone in. "Group shot!"

But I just stand there, blinking my eyes and breathing fast, like I'm waking up from a nightmare. One where a monster is chasing me, but no matter how fast I run, I can't get away.

I need air.

Now.

I throw the agate down.

And bolt out the door.

"Ida!" Alex calls as I rush past her and Pete. "Where are you going?"

I glance back. "I . . . I . . . I lost something," I say. "At the beach. I'll be right back."

I turn away and hurry down the path. Past Hawk. Past Sparrow. Wishing I had gotten dressed first. Or at least grabbed my towel. I must look crazy, flip-flopping through the woods in nothing but a two-piece. If the boys see me, they'll start singing about my underwear again.

But when your last best friend—the one who *ditched* you—shows up out of the blue, you don't stick around for the welcome back party.

"Hey, Ida! Wait up!"

I glance back again and see Pete, the maintenance guy, speed-walking toward me.

I flip-flop faster.

"Hey," he says, catching up to me. "I'm an expert at finding lost stuff. Beach towels. Sandals. Sunscreen. It all goes in a lost-and-found box.

Unless it's valuable, like a camera." He looks at me. "Did you lose something valuable?"

"No," I reply, speeding up.

For a big guy, he's awfully fast. We pass the dining hall. Kids and counselors are already gathering for supper. They stare at us as we head toward the lake—a hairy man carrying a toilet plunger and a little kid wearing mostly just her birthday suit.

Thankfully, the beach is empty when we get there. I hop from the stone wall to the sand, then turn to Pete. "You can go," I say, as coolly as I can, even though most of me is on fire. "I can find what I lost by myself."

Pete stands above me on the grassy ledge. "Sure thing," he says. "It's just . . . you're not allowed on the beach without a staffer. Sorry. We've got rules."

I sigh and look around. Then I scoot my blue butt up onto the stone wall, flip-flops dangling. "I'm not *on* the beach now," I say.

Pete nods. He points to a small shed near a vegetable garden that's next to the dining hall. *Maintenance Shack* is printed on a sign above the door.

"That's my executive office," he says with a grin. "Holler if you need anything."

I stare at the lake as Pete walks away. Listening to the water lap the shore again and again and again. *Elizabeth Evans is back,* I think to myself. *She's back . . . she's back . . . she's back . . .*

"Ida! There you are!"

I turn and see Stacey, running up to me with the shirt and shorts I left on my bed. She sits down on the stone wall, catching her breath. "Alex let me run ahead. I grabbed your clothes. It's time for supper."

"Thanks," I say, slipping the clothes on over my swimsuit. "You're the best friend ever."

"Takes one to know one!" Stacey does a teasey grin. Then her face goes serious. "Is everything okay? Alex said you lost something."

I shake my head. "I just freaked out a little."

Stacey nods. "Over Liz, right?"

I nod back. "I can't believe she just showed up like that. Acting like we should all be glad she's here. Dancing around in those dumb cowboy boots. Wearing the friendship bracelet *I* made for her. What does she think? We're still best friends?"

"Maybe she wants to make up," Stacey offers. "You know, for not writing to you."

I give her a blank look. "Are you serious? You think I should take her back, just like that?"

"That's not what I meant," Stacey replies. "I'm not choosing sides, so don't be mad at me. It's just . . . maybe there's a reason she never wrote to you. When I moved to Purdee, it took my mom forever to get e-mail. And texting? Ha. I didn't even have a cell phone back then. And I never thought to get my old BFF's street address before I moved."

"Elizabeth had mine," I say, my voice crackling. "It was on every letter I wrote to her."

Stacey is quiet for a minute. Then she stands up, brushing grass off her shorts. "I'm just saying, give Liz a chance to explain before you decide she's not worth keeping."

"I've already decided," I say. "She's not."

Stacey sighs. Holds her hand out to me.

I let her pull me up.

Bong! Bong! Bong!

We look toward the dining hall and see Connor pulling on a rope that's connected to an old-fashioned bell. He lets Rusty, Joey, Quinn, and Tom take a turn too.

Cabin doors slam. Voices echo off the water. Campers appear like ants at a picnic. Connor jumps up on a bench by the dining hall doors. A couple other counselors hop up too. "Gather in!" he shouts. "Time to rock this place!"

Someone hands Connor a guitar and he starts jamming. The other counselors clap along, shout-singing a song.

Camp Meadowlark! Camp Meadowlark!
Where we love to sing and chirp,
And occasionally burp!
Camp Meadowlark! Camp Meadowlark!
Sure, the cabins creak,
But the rowboats seldom leak!
Camp Meadowlark! Camp Meadowlark!
The lake is never dry,
And our bracelets always tie!
Camp Meadowlark! Camp Meadowlark!
The counselors are neat,
Please excuse their stinky feet!
Camp Meadowlark! Camp Meadowlurk!

Where friendship makes us strong,
As we swim and hike along!
Camp Meadowlark! Camp Meadowlark . . .

"Look," Stacey says. "There're the other girls."

Alex comes around the corner of the dining hall, swinging hands with Meeka and Jolene.

Jenna shuffles along behind them, writing something on her clipboard.

Randi takes a spot by Rusty and the other boys. They play air guitar and shout-sing along with Connor and the others.

Brooke sees Nat and Emillie and dashes to them like a tack to magnets.

Elizabeth weaves through the crowd until she's right next to me and Stacey. "Hi!" she says, all breathless and cheery. "Where'd you go?"

I pretend I can't hear her over the singing.

"Um . . ." Stacey says, when she realizes I'm not going to answer. "We took a detour."

"It's so bizarre to see everyone again," Elizabeth prattles on, like I'm interested in what she has to say. "I can't believe Brooke brought a *crown*! Wait . . . yes I can." She giggles. "You missed her modeling it for me. And Jenna? She's making a *seating chart* for supper. Too funny! Some things never change."

Elizabeth links arms with me. "Who cares, though, right? I'm sitting by you no matter what. I've got gobs of stuff to tell you!"

I snatch my arm away. "*I* care," I say. "And things *have* changed. Jenna's my friend now. I'll sit where she wants me to sit, and I'm pretty sure it won't be by *you*."

Stacey mouths a silent *Wow*.

So does Elizabeth.

The song ends.

The dining hall doors open.

Everyone starts crowding in.

I grab Stacey's hand and we get swept along.

When I glance back, Elizabeth Evans is a million miles away.

Good.

Chapter

7

After supper, Alex takes us for a walk around the main path at camp. It connects everything—girls' cabins, dining hall, garden, beach, campfire ring, crafts cottage, boys' cabins, ball field. The path must look like a big circle to the birds flying over us, with the lake hugging it on one side and the woods hugging it on the other. Alex points toward the woods as we approach them. "We'll go on a campout Thursday night!"

Meeka gulps, peering through the trees. "But the boys say a monster lives out there."

Alex does a half smile and takes Meeka's hand. "Don't worry about that old monster," she says reassuringly. "He's no match for a bunch of Chickadees . . . right?"

"Right!" Randi says. "And if worst comes to

worst, we'll dip Brooke in chocolate sauce and use her as a human sacrifice."

"Ha-ha," Brooke says. "Very funny."

"Some people say there are ghosts at the Grand Canyon," Elizabeth puts in. "But my family camped there anyway. It's in Arizona, which is right next to New Mexico, where I lived."

Jenna grunts. "Thank you for the geography lesson, but you're not in New Mexico anymore."

"And we're not your family," I add.

Jenna grins.

Stacey shoots me a look. Then she gives Elizabeth a smile. "Sure we are, Liz," she says. "We're a family of chickadees!"

"Birds live in flocks, not families," Jenna points out.

"We *are* a family," Alex cuts in. "Just a different kind." She stops suddenly and looks into the woods.

"What is it?" Meeka asks nervously. "Do you see the monster?"

"No," Alex replies. "I just thought of something I want to show you."

Jenna looks over the checklist on her clipboard. "But we've seen everything."

"Not quite," Alex replies. "There's something new. Pete built it." She steps off the path and into the woods, motioning for us to follow her.

"I *hate* new things," Jenna grumbles as we trample through brush and weave between the trees. "Why can't things stay the same?"

"Most things don't," Elizabeth says, pausing to hold a branch aside as me and Jenna pass through. "Trust me."

Jenna glares at her. "I wasn't talking to you, Liz*butt*. I was talking to Ida."

Elizabeth lets the branch whip back into place, just missing Jenna. "Maybe you're right," she says crisply. "I know *one* thing hasn't changed."

Jenna stops and squints at her. "What?"

Elizabeth clomps ahead in her cowboy boots. "You're still calling me names."

Jenna shakes her head as we watch her go. "She's loonier than a loon. Look at her. Red boots. Plaid shorts. Goofy glasses. This is *nature* camp, not *clown* camp."

"Just ignore her," I say, taking Jenna's hand. "Then she'll leave us alone."

A minute later, we enter a small clearing in

the woods. A wooden platform stands at the center of it. Almost as tall as me, and a little bit wider.

"What's this supposed to be?" Brooke asks, climbing onto the platform and doing an awkward twirl. "A stage for squirrels?"

"It's not a stage," Alex says. "It's a trust fall platform."

Jenna puffs. "What's it good for?"

"For building trust," Alex replies. "The person standing on the platform falls off. Everyone catches her."

"She just . . . falls?" I ask.

Alex nods. "Stiff and straight, like a domino."

"Cool," Randi says.

"*Not* cool." Brooke hops down. "I'd get broken to bits."

"Not if you trust us to catch you," Alex replies.

Brooke crosses her arms. "What if you *don't*?"

Alex smiles. "What if we *do*?"

Brooke snorts and turns away. "D-U-M *dumb*."

Alex looks around our group. "Who wants to give it a try?"

Everyone gets busy studying their toenail

polish. Except Elizabeth. She's studying *me*. I pretend not to study her back.

"We didn't have to do this last year," Jenna grumbles again.

"You don't have to do it this year either," Alex says. "Only if you want to."

Randi steps forward. "I'll do it," she says.

Brooke's eyes go wide. "Are you crazy?"

Randi scrambles onto the platform. "Crazy or not, here I come. Catch me, okay?"

I gulp. Randi's the biggest girl in our class. None of us have ever caught her before. Not even in tag.

Alex lines us up in two rows under the platform, facing each other.

Shoulder to shoulder.

Arms out.

Elbows bent.

Palms up.

Brooke snickers, looking up and down our row of twig-thin arms. "She is so dead."

We all fidget and nod.

"Randi trusts you," Alex says firmly. "Now you need to trust each other."

She looks up at Randi. "Stiff and straight," she reminds her.

Randi nods. "Like a domino."

Then she turns around.

Straightens her back.

Locks her knees.

Crosses her arms.

"Falling!" she shouts.

"Fall away!" Alex replies.

Randi tips back on her heels.

Whoosh!

A moment later, she's lying in our arms.

"Hi, guys!" she says, smiling up at us. "Thought I'd drop in!"

"Ohmy*gosh*!" Brooke says. "We did it!"

"I knew you could," Alex says.

"Fun!" Stacey cries. "Me next!"

She climbs onto the platform.

A moment later, Stacey falls into our arms too.

"Hey, we're getting good at this," Jolene says.

"I wish I would have brought my camera," Meeka puts in.

"Anyone else?" Alex asks as we set Stacey on her feet.

"I hope not," Brooke says, rubbing her arms. "I'll probably have bruises tomorrow. Nat and Emillie will think I'm a sports freak."

Elizabeth starts to raise her hand.

Jenna steps in, blocking her. "I'll go." She kicks her clipboard aside and climbs onto the platform. "But after this, we'll need a schedule. It can't be alphabetical since Randi fell first." She pauses, thinking. "But she *is* tallest. Then Stacey. Then me. The falling schedule will be according to height."

"Then consider me invisible," Brooke says, "because I'm not falling off that thing."

Jenna turns around and straightens her back. "If you're on my schedule, Brooke, you're falling."

Beep! Beep! Beep!

Jenna pushes a button on her watch. "Quick!" she says. "Catch me. It's time for campfire."

Just like that, Jenna falls. We scramble to catch her.

"Are you going to fall?" Elizabeth asks me as Jenna grabs her clipboard and hurries to lead the way back to Chickadee.

I shrug, and head after the others.

But Elizabeth takes my arm, stopping me. "I will if you will." She makes her eyes go all serious behind her glasses.

I make my eyes go all serious too. Because I've heard her make that promise lots of times before.

When we were finally tall enough to ride the big roller coaster at the fair.

When we discovered her sister's diary.

When we wondered what Champ's dog biscuits tasted like.

But, most of all, she made that promise when she asked me to be her best friend forever. Right before she moved away and wrote to me exactly zero times.

I wiggle my arm free and walk away.

I brush the marshmallows out of my teeth after campfire, change into my pajamas, and join the other girls in Alex's room. She's showing Stacey and Brooke some of the jewelry she's made.

Randi and Jolene are sitting on Alex's bed, posing with her stuffed animals while Meeka takes pictures.

Jenna is sitting on the floor, using some of

Alex's markers to draw a border around the trust fall schedule on her clipboard.

"Do you have any paper with lines?" Elizabeth asks, looking over Jenna's shoulder at her clipboard.

Jenna looks up. "Yes," she replies.

"Can I borrow some?"

Jenna looks down. "No. I only brought enough for me."

"I have paper," Alex says, glancing over from her desk. "Lined . . . blank . . . whatever!" She opens a drawer. "Help yourself."

"Thanks," Elizabeth replies, taking a few sheets of notepaper back to her bunk.

"Ida's desk is stuffed with paper too," Stacey says, holding a beaded hoop up to her earlobe and looking at herself in Alex's mirror. "She's a great artist. You should see her sketchbook!"

All the girls nod.

I do a shy smile.

"Cool!" Alex says to me. "I lead crafts every day. We draw and paint and make stuff out of beads and glitter. You should come!"

I give her a smile.

Brooke gasps, dropping one of the necklaces she's trying on. "Did you say *glitter*? I'm the *queen* of glitter!"

"The more the merrier!" Alex replies.

Brooke squeals. "I'll bring Nat and Emillie!"

I sigh.

Alex starts putting her jewelry away. "Time for bed, girls. Get snuggled in. I'll read you a story before lights-out."

Brooke sniffs, putting the necklaces back in a box. "We're too old for bedtime stories."

Alex picks up a flashlight and a book. "You're never too old," she replies.

"Make it spooky!" Randi says, hopping up from Alex's bed.

"Not *too* spooky," Meeka adds, clicking off her camera and following the others to their bunks.

"I'd love to see your sketchbook sometime, Ida," Alex says, dimming the lights.

"Maybe," I reply, and hurry to my bunk too while she gets ready to read.

I unzip my sleeping bag, squish George to one side, and climb in. But something pokes me in the back.

I roll over and turn on my flashlight.

A rock is lying there.

Red with white swirls.

"It's the agate me and Jenna found," I whisper to George. "But how did it—"

Then I see a crumpled note next to the agate. I pick it up and read the words to George.

Ida,

Here's the rock you dropped.

I know you meant it for me, but that was before you knew who I was.

So I'm giving it back.

Liz

"Who are you talking to?" Jenna pokes her head over the edge of her bunk.

I hide the note with George. And hold the rock up for Jenna to see. "It's the agate we found," I whisper.

Jenna glances over at Elizabeth's bunk. I glance too. Elizabeth's tucked inside her sleeping bag, staring at the empty bunk above her, listening to Alex read about some girl who lives with wolves.

"Keep it," Jenna tells me. "Agates are rare."
Then she rolls away again.

*Jenna's right. Agates don't show up very often.
But I don't want some rare rock around to remind
me of Elizabeth either.*

I slip out of bed and tiptoe to the wastebasket
that's by Elizabeth's bunk.

First, I toss the note.

Then, I drop the rock.

Plunk!

I crawl back into bed.

Elizabeth rolls away.

Chapter

8

Monday morning, I wake up to the sound of my dad's coffee grinder rattling downstairs in the kitchen.

But when I open my eyes, I see Jenna's bunk above me and remember I'm a long way from home.

I hear the sound again.

Ratta-tat-tat-tat-tat-tat!

Rolling over, I lift the curtain that covers the open window between my bunk and Elizabeth's. Sunshine peeks through the trees. A woodpecker is tapping on one of them.

"What's for breakfast?" I mumble to him sleepily. "Bark juice and scrambled beetles?"

He cocks his bright red head. Then starts tapping again.

I look around the room. Seven sleeping lumps.

Scattered sweatshirts and jeans. A jumble of flip-flops and swimsuits on the floor. I crane my neck and see that Alex's bed is empty. She must have gone for her run. She told us she goes every morning.

I lie back on my pillow, pat the George-shaped lump that's burrowed next to me, and look over at Elizabeth's sleeping face and messy hair.

Without her glasses, she looks like the Elizabeth I used to know. The one I could talk to without any words. Not in a magic way, like me and George can. Just in the way friends do when they send messages to each other with their eyes. Stacey is good at it. Jenna too, sometimes.

But you can't send eye messages between Purdee, Wisconsin, and Albuquerque, New Mexico. No one can see that far. Not even hawks.

Elizabeth shifts in her sleep. Her sleeping bag slips partway off the mattress. One of her arms slips too. The faded blue friendship bracelet I made for her last year dangles from it. So does the wristband Alex gave her for swimming. Tadpole pink, just like mine. When Randi asked Elizabeth how come she doesn't want to swim to the raft, Elizabeth just said, "There's more to do by the shore."

Like what? Dodge snapping turtles?

Her fingers twitch and I see a chip of orange polish sparkle on each nail.

I frown and sit up a notch.

She hates orange, I think to George. *It always reminds her of real oranges, which are hard to peel and have those sticky white strings.*

I lean forward, squinting to see if her fingernails really are painted orange or if I need glasses too.

My bed creaks.

Elizabeth's eyes pop open.

So do mine.

She blinks a few times. Yawns. Rubs away the sleep. "What are you looking at?" she whispers to me.

"Um..." I reply, shrinking back. "I thought...I saw something. Under your bed. A mouse maybe. Or a squirrel."

Elizabeth pulls her sleeping bag off the floor. "Really?" she says, reaching for her glasses.

I nod. "They sneak in sometimes. Looking for food."

"But there's no food in here," Elizabeth whispers. She puts on her glasses and looks around. "Is there?"

I do a very casual snort. "Duh-*no*." Then I force myself not to look at Brooke's backpack. Elizabeth doesn't know about the snacks. I want to keep it that way.

But, sometimes, the more you try not to do something, the more you can't help but do it. My eyes dart to the backpack on Brooke's bottom bunk. It's as plump as a Thanksgiving turkey. When I look at Elizabeth again, her eyes are fixed on it too. The only thing in the room that's still zipped up tight.

Elizabeth turns to me and does a sly grin, like she's Sherlock Holmes or something. "There *is* food in here," she whispers. "That's why Jenna spazzed last night at the campfire when Jolene wanted to save a marshmallow for the chipmunk she saw on our cabin steps. What was it Jenna said to Jolene? Oh yeah. 'Between you and Brooke, Chickadee is going to turn into Noah's Ark.'"

She studies Brooke's backpack again, still grinning. "You guys brought snacks!"

I do an *I-don't-know-what-you're-talking-about* look.

Elizabeth does an *I-know-I'm-right* look back.

I squint. "You better not tell."

She grins bigger. "Why not?"

"Because those snacks are none of your business. Because friends don't tell on each other."

She leans in. Her grin tightens. "So we're friends now, huh? You've got a funny way of showing it."

"I wasn't talking about—"

Beep! Beep! Bee—!

Jenna shifts above me. The beeping stops. A moment later, two fuzzy braids hang over the edge of her bed. So does Jenna's sleepy face.

"Rise and shine," she says in a groggy voice. "Breakfast in thirty minutes." Then she lumbers down and starts waking up the other girls.

I turn back to Elizabeth, but she's already out of bed, pulling clothes from her suitcase. She ducks into the bathroom.

I scramble out of my sleeping bag and find the notepaper my mom packed for me in case I get the sudden urge to write a letter home. I grab a gel pen, bite off the cap, and start scribbling what I didn't finish saying to her. All capital letters, so she'll know I mean business.

I WASN'T TALKING ABOUT ME.
I WAS TALKING ABOUT THE OTHER GIRLS.
IF YOU WANT THEM TO BE YOUR FRIENDS,
THEN YOU BETTER NOT TELL!

I drop the note on Elizabeth's bed, grab my clothes, and stomp to the bathroom.

"Whoa," Randi says, inching away as I get in line behind her. "Someone's not a morning person."

Stacey looks over from her bunk. Her hair is so poufy, eagles could build a nest in it. "What's wrong?" she asks me.

"Nothing," I grumble. "I just got up on the wrong side of the bed. The *Elizabeth* side."

"Why? Does Liz snore?" Meeka asks, straightening her sleeping bag.

"No," I reply. "She just talks too much."

"In her sleep?" Jolene asks.

I shake my head. "In her *awake*."

"So switch bunks." Jenna gets in line behind

me with her towel and toothbrush. "Take the one above her. Then you'll be closer to me."

"Yeah, come up to *my* level," Brooke says, still lounging on her top bunk. "The view is fantabulous!"

The bathroom door opens. Elizabeth steps out. Everyone goes hush-hush.

Elizabeth looks around suspiciously. "What did I miss?" she asks.

"It doesn't concern you," Jenna snips.

"Ida's moving," Brooke tells her. "To a top bunk." Then she slides down, grabs some clothes from the tangled heap on her bottom bunk, and slips into the bathroom ahead of Randi.

"Hey!" Randi shouts, pounding on the door. "No cuts!"

Brooke clicks the lock.

"Hold this," I say to Jenna, handing her my bathroom stuff. Then I march past Elizabeth, gather up my sleeping bag, and throw it onto the bed above hers.

George grunts when he hits the mattress. Maybe he's not a morning monkey. Or maybe he's not a fan of moving.

But this is *my* decision.

It's my turn to leave Elizabeth Evans behind.

I get back in line and take my stuff from Jenna. "I feel better already," I say to her, hoping Elizabeth hears me.

Jenna nods. "I knew you would."

Brooke bursts from the bathroom a minute later dressed in a bright orange cami and orange-striped shorts. Her hair is brushed long and smooth. She strikes a pose.

Randi scowls and shoves past her, slamming the bathroom door.

Brooke scoffs. "How R-U-D *rude*." Then she struts around the cabin, modeling her orange outfit. "It's *new*," she tells us.

"Nice!" Elizabeth says as Brooke step-turns in front of her. "I *love* orange, see?" She wiggles her sparkly orange fingernails at Brooke.

Brooke gives Elizabeth an approving smile. "There's hope for you yet, Liz*butt* Evans."

I just shake my head, watching Elizabeth giggle as Brooke glamour poses around her. *Buddying up to Brooke? Pretending to like orange best? She must be desperate to get friends.*

Brooke twirls back to her bunk.

Elizabeth sets down her stuff.

She sees the note on her bed.

Picks it up.

Starts to read.

I watch out of the corner of my eye, waiting for her face to pinch when she finishes. When she realizes it won't work to buddy up to *me*.

"Your turn, Ida," Jenna says as Randi comes out of the bathroom. She's wearing a big boyish T-shirt. It's almost as long as her cargo shorts. *Sarcasm is my specialty* is printed across it.

Brooke glances over. Wrinkles her nose at the T-shirt. "Where did you get *that*?" she asks.

Randi puffs up her chest and grins. "Swiped it from my brother. I got a whole collection. Wanna borrow one?"

"*No* thank you," Brooke snips. She straightens the straps on her orange top. "And please don't sit by me at breakfast."

Randi snaps her fingers. "Darn."

"Go, Ida!" Jenna says, nudging me impatiently toward the bathroom. "The bell is going to ring in seventeen minutes!"

"Yes, please do hurry, Ida *dear*," Brooke adds, brushing out her already brushed hair. "I have places to go and people to impress."

I step into the bathroom, glancing back at Elizabeth.

She's by the wastebasket now.

Crumpling my note into a hard paper pebble.

She pitches it into the trash.

Plink!

Then she looks at me.

Does that annoying smile-grin.

"Ha-ha, beat you!" Rusty shouts fifteen minutes later as Alex leads us up to the dining hall. Quinn, Joey, and Tom are there too, standing near the door with their counselor, Connor. Pajama pants. Wrinkled T-shirts. Crusty eyes. Messy hair. They look the same as always.

Brooke crosses her arms and tilts her hips. "Haven't you ever heard of *ladies first*?"

"Yep," Rusty replies. "Show us where they are, and we'll let them take cuts."

All the boys snort.

Brooke squints.

"Hi, Elizabeth!" Tom says. "Good to see you again."

Elizabeth smiles. "Same to you, Tom."

"Did you come to camp with Ida?" he asks.

I stiffen.

"No," Elizabeth replies quickly. "I came alone."

Quinn scratches his head, confused. "You guys know each other?"

"Duh, Quinn," Brooke cuts in. "It's *Liz Evans.* She used to go to our school. Now she's moving back."

Tom perks up. "You are?"

Elizabeth nods. "I already have, actually. My parents are painting my new bedroom this week!"

"Ooo . . . what color?" Jolene asks.

"Blue!" Elizabeth replies.

"Knew it," I mumble.

"You should text your parents immediately," Brooke says. "Tell them blue is *out,* orange is *in.*" She flicks back her hair from her orange top. "Then I can plan an orange-themed sleepover!" She thinks for a moment. "Everyone will wear orange, of course. And bring orange snacks. Gummy bears . . . cheese puffs . . . orange soda. We can even write the invitations on actual *oranges*! And call it the *Orange You Glad Liz Moved Back Snooze-Fest*!"

Brooke squeals with excitement. She loves to plan parties. Once, when a soccer ball split Meeka's lip in phys ed, Brooke hosted the *Don't Give Me Any Lip Masquerade*. We all had to wear costumes. And lip sync to Brooke's favorite songs. Then we ate banana splits. Poor Meeka had to put hers in the blender first so she could sip it through a straw.

"Sounds fun!" Elizabeth says all nicey-nice to Brooke. "But my parents already bought blue paint. And I didn't bring a cell phone."

Brooke does a dramatic sigh. "Too bad, so sad. We'll have to settle for the *Blue Bedroom Bash*. Not nearly as imaginative as orange."

Quinn studies Elizabeth, rapping a knuckle against his forehead. "Nope. Still not computing."

Jenna rolls her eyes. "How can you not remember her, Quinn? She built that dumb valentines box in third grade. The *Mountain of Love*?"

Elizabeth twitches when Jenna says that. Her eyes dart to me, then away again. "It was called the *Volcano of Love,*" Elizabeth corrects her.

Jenna's cheeks flash red. She hates being wrong. She hates it more when someone else is right.

"Hey, I remember that volcano," Tom chimes in. "It was made out of papier-mâché. You had to lift the lava cork to put the valentines inside. Genius."

Elizabeth gives Tom another smile.

Jenna steams.

"I didn't move to Purdee until spring that year," Quinn says. He looks at Elizabeth. "Sorry, but I don't remember you. Third grade is kind of a blur. It sucks to move."

Elizabeth nods. "I know."

Now she and *Quinn* exchange smiles. The kind that says *We know something the others don't.*

The kind that makes you instant friends.

My stomach prickles. Quinn is *my* friend, not hers.

I look around for Alex. "How much longer until we eat?" I say loudly, trying to change the subject and stop all the smiling that's going on.

Alex looks over from talking with Connor.

"Soon," she replies, checking her watch. "We could sing a song while we wait."

Nobody exactly squeals with excitement. It's hard to get enthused about singing when you haven't had your breakfast yet. And when your mouth is watering from the scent of bacon in the air.

"Finish the story you started last night," Joey says to Connor. "I'm dying to know if the Meadowlark Monster ate you and Pete!"

Jenna snorts. "If a monster ate them, they wouldn't be here."

"Good point," Joey says. He looks at Connor again. "Permanently maimed, then. Please?"

Connor rubs his chin. I can hear his whiskers waking up. "Okay, but I better start at the beginning, or the girls will be lost."

"Too late for that," Rusty says. "But go ahead."

"It was a dark and stormy night," Connor begins in a spooky voice, like we're sitting around a crackling campfire instead of standing in the soft morning sun. "Pete and I were heading back to camp through the woods, when suddenly, there he was! *The Meadowlark Monster!*"

"Tell them what he looked like," Joey says.

We all scoot in.

"He was as big as a bear." Connor holds his arms out wide. "And his fur was matted with dirt and leaves, like he'd just crawled out of a *grave*."

Meeka gulps.

Jenna huffs and checks her watch.

"He only had one eye left, but it *glowed* enough for two. And when he howled"—Connor does a howl that could seriously make you pee your pants if you hadn't just gone to the bathroom—"it shook the trees!"

Other campers look over.

Meeka gulps again and squeezes my arm.

"He chased us through the woods, quick as lightning, snatching at us with his huge hands."

"He's got hands?" Quinn asks. "He didn't last night."

"Um . . . yeah . . ." Connor says, the words stumbling out, ". . . *webbed* hands . . . covered with *slime*." He glances at Alex. She rolls her eyes. "Pete and I thought we were goners. But then, we remembered the one thing monsters hate most."

He pauses, pushing back his floppy orange hair.

"This is where he left off last night," Tom whispers.

"Tell us!" Joey cries. "What do monsters hate most?"

A smile flits between Connor and Alex.

Connor leans in. "The thing that monsters hate most . . ." he whispers, ". . . is *singing*."

Our faces sag.

"That's *it*?" Rusty says. "Singing?"

Connor nods. "That's why monsters only come out at night. When the birds are asleep."

Jenna does a sassy smirk. "So what did you sing? The Camp Meadowlark theme song?"

Connor shakes his head. "We needed something bigger than that."

" 'The Star-Spangled Banner'?" Quinn offers.

"Nope," Connor says. "Bigger. We sang *opera*."

Jolene giggles. "That fancy music?"

Connor nods. Then he cups his hands around his mouth and tips up his chin. *"Figaro . . . Figaro . . . Figarooooo!"* he bellows, like an opera star. Not a very good one.

Connor waits until we unplug our ears. Then he says, "The monster took off and we haven't seen him since. The end."

The boys applaud.

"Dumb," Jenna says. "Singing wouldn't scare away a monster."

Connor gives Jenna a very serious look. "Never doubt the power of a well-placed song," he tells her. "Especially when you sing it with your friends."

Jenna steps closer to me.

Rusty tips up his chin, just like Connor. *"Figaro . . . Figaro . . . Figarooooo!"* he belts out.

All the boys join in.

All us girls plug our ears.

Chapter

9

Alex stays at the dining hall after breakfast for a staff meeting while the rest of us head back to Chickadee. We're supposed to clean it up. The group that keeps their cabin the cleanest wins the Silver Paddle Award at the end of the week. It's really just an old canoe paddle that somebody painted silver. *Cleanest Cabin* is printed across it. But the way the counselors cheered when Connor brought it out—pumping it in the air like a football player who just won a Super Bowl trophy—made you believe that even an old canoe paddle could be worth fighting for.

"We have *got* to win the Silver Paddle," Jenna tells us as we hike back to Chickadee.

"Yep," Randi says. "Do or die."

"What's the big deal?" Brooke asks. "It's just

a stupid painted paddle. It doesn't even have any glitter."

Jenna looks at Brooke like she just suggested that gravity is stupid. "The group that wins the Silver Paddle gets their picture taken, Brooke. They put it on display for everyone to see."

"I could take the picture!" Meeka says, pulling out her camera and clicking a shot as we walk along.

"No, you couldn't," Stacey says helpfully. "When we win the Silver Paddle, you'll be in the picture too!"

"Oh, yeah!" Meeka says, clicking a shot of Stacey.

Brooke flicks back her hair. "Nobody told me it would involve a photo shoot. Fine. We'll win the stupid paddle."

Elizabeth rushes ahead to Chickadee and holds open the door for everyone, like she's trying to earn a Brownie badge or something.

"You can't win a Silver Paddle for holding open a door," I tell her.

"I'm not trying to win anything," she says as everyone files past. "I'm trying to be *nice*."

She narrows her eyes into slits behind her glasses.

"Keep practicing," I reply. Then I bump past her and head inside.

We get busy cleaning. Randi and Elizabeth sweep. Meeka and Jolene straighten suitcases. Stacey sorts flip-flops. Jenna wipes toothpaste off the bathroom sink. I finish moving to my new bunk. Sketchbook. Pencils. Pens. The notepaper from Mom. A flashlight, in case George gets scared at night.

I climb up and get everything organized, being careful to keep the pens and pencils away from the crack that's between the bunk and the wall. I don't want them to fall through.

I don't want *me* to fall through either.

So I do a little test.

But the only part of me that fits through the crack is my arm.

Good. The last thing I want to do is fall on top of Elizabeth Evans.

"I can only do soft chores," Brooke announces. She's sitting crisscross-applesauce on her top bunk, fluffing a pillow. "Otherwise, I might damage a nail. That would be tragic because I forgot to pack extra polish."

Randi sweeps around Brooke's bunk, mumbling something about damaged brains. Her broom accidentally knocks Brooke's fat backpack to the floor.

Thunk!

"Hey!" Brooke snaps at Randi. "Be careful. You're breaking the chips!"

Randi hoists the backpack onto Brooke's bottom bunk again. "Then we better eat them before they go bad." She looks around the room at everyone. "Snack time!"

Elizabeth stops sweeping. "Oh?" she says, all innocent. "You brought snacks?"

She shoots that grin at me.

"Duh," Brooke says. "What did you think? We'd starve all week?"

Jenna peeks out from the bathroom, a wad of toothpastey paper towel in her hand. She looks at her watch. "It's nine thirty-seven in the morning. That's way too early for snacks."

"It's never too early," Randi replies. She pokes the backpack with the end of her broom. "Let's eat!"

Brooke hops down. "Fine, but the snacks have to last four more days. I'll ration them out." She unzips the backpack. Chips, gum, cookies, cherry whips, Choco Chunks—it all spills onto her bottom bunk like lava from a volcano. A real one, not some dumb valentines box.

Jenna steps up. "But you *promised* not to eat in the cabin."

"I had my fingers crossed," Brooke replies, "so that promise doesn't count. Besides, one teeny bag of potato chips isn't going to attract anything bigger than a fly. We'll split it eight ways." She rips open a shiny yellow bag. "Leftovers go to me since I'm the brains behind this operation."

Randi mumbles something about brains again. But Brooke is too busy concentrating on counting out potato chips to pay attention to Randi. A minute later, everyone is munching. Even Jenna. It's hard to follow the rules when a pair of potato chips are staring you in the eye.

"Look!" Stacey says, licking her salty fingers and pointing at Elizabeth. "Liz got a green one. That's good luck!"

"It is?" Elizabeth pinches up the potato chip she's holding. Its edge is as green as a shark wristband.

"No it's not," Jenna says, rubbing her greasy hand on her shorts. "Green means *bad* luck."

"No refunds," Brooke quips, shaking crumbs from the chip bag. She sucks them up like a vacuum cleaner. Then she tucks the empty bag back inside her pack, stuffs in the other candy, and zips it shut.

"That's *it*?" Randi says. "I only got two chips!"

"I told you," Brooke replies. "We have to make the snacks last."

Elizabeth steps closer to the window while Brooke and Randi argue over snack rations, turning the green chip in the sunlight like it's edged with emeralds.

I watch her, nibbling and thinking about what just happened.

Not the green potato chip part.

The part where Brooke said, "We'll split it *eight* ways."

She didn't even need to stop and count us up.

She just knew.

Elizabeth sticks the green chip in her mouth and munches away.

☙❧

"Crayons? Glitter? Pinecones? Why is everything at this camp for little kids?" Emillie wrinkles her nose at the baskets of craft supplies that are sitting on the tables in the crafts cottage when we get there later on Monday morning. Brooke made us stop at Hawk cabin to invite Emillie and Nat along. *Us* meaning me, Stacey, and Elizabeth. Stacey invited *her*. Randi and Jenna went to kickball. Meeka and Jolene went on a nature hike.

Nat walks over to one of the tables. It's covered with white paper. *Draw on me!* is written across it in friendly print. The other table is set up the same way.

She picks up a crayon. Sniffs it like it's skunk scented. "And to think I used to *love* this kind of stuff." She draws a frowny face on the table and then plops down on one of its long benches.

Emillie sits across from her on the other bench. She takes a pinecone from a basket, breaks off a spike, and flicks it at Nat. "Told you we should have gone to kickball," she says. "At least there would be boys there."

The door creaks open.

Tom walks in. "Hi!" he says, giving us a friendly wave.

Emillie rolls her eyes. "I mean *real* boys."

Brooke shoots a look at Tom. "What are *you* doing here?" She scoots in next to Nat. "Art is for *girls*."

Tom cocks his head. "Was Picasso a girl? Was van Gogh? Was Monet?"

Brooke squints. "Who knows, who cares, Tom *Thumb*."

Emillie snickers. "Good one." She reaches across the table and gives Brooke a high five.

Nat gives her one too.

Brooke smiles so big I can see her molars.

Tom sits at the other table.

Elizabeth joins him.

Brooke pulls Stacey in next to her.

"No vacancy," Emillie says to me, stretching her long, tan legs across the bench she's sitting on.

More campers come in. They pause, look at Nat and Emillie, and then head to the other table.

When I get there, the only spot left is across from Elizabeth. I don't want to spend a whole hour not looking at her.

I glance at the door. "Maybe I'll play kickball."

"But you love art," Tom says, picking up a brown crayon and sketching a tree on the table paper.

"And you *hate* kickball," Elizabeth adds, drawing a purple rabbit under Tom's tree.

"No I don't," I tell her, even though I do.

Elizabeth glances up. "We used to hide behind that cow hedge on the schoolyard when our teacher made us play."

"Bessie," Tom says, drawing leaves on his tree. "I've hidden behind her too."

"It never worked, though," Elizabeth continues. "Our teacher always found us and hauled us back to the game."

I lift my chin. "Things change," I say in my icy voice. "I don't hide behind cow hedges anymore. Neither do my *friends*."

Tom looks up. He does a fake shiver. "Brrrr," he says. "I should have worn a sweatshirt. It's chilly in here."

Elizabeth draws a fluffy white tail on her purple rabbit, which is dumb because the paper is white and it barely shows up. "Well then, maybe you *should* play kickball. With your *friends*."

My eyes turn into ice picks. So do Elizabeth's. We poke them at each other.

"Yep," Tom mumbles. "Definitely sweatshirt weather."

The door opens. Alex sidesteps in, carrying a stack of cardboard. "Sorry I'm late!" she says. "Pete was helping me cut up boxes so we'll have something to set our pinecone critters on."

"Oh, goodie!" Emillie squeals, patty-caking her hands like a baby. "Pinecone critters!"

Brooke and Nat laugh. They start playing patty-cake too.

"I'll help," Stacey says, getting up quickly and taking the cardboard from Alex. Stacey's not a fan of patty-cake.

"I'll help too," I say, joining Stacey. Because, right now, I'm not a fan of sitting down.

"Thanks!" Alex gives us a smile.

We hand around the cardboard slowly, and then set the extra by some shelves that are loaded with more art supplies. Paper. Beads. Paint in every kind of color. Even glow-in-the-dark.

"Do you want to switch seats?" Stacey asks me

in a low voice, glancing at Brooke, Nat, and Emillie. They're playing table hockey with a pinecone.

"I like pinecone hockey even less than kickball," I say to Stacey. "And I like sitting by Nat and Emillie even less than sitting by Elizabeth Evans."

Stacey sighs. "Don't blame you," she says, and trudges back to Brooke.

I plop down across from Elizabeth.

Elizabeth looks up. Blinks, all innocent. "How was kickball?"

Tom snickers.

I pick up a red crayon. "Your tree could use some apples," I say to Tom, ignoring Elizabeth.

"Be my guest," Tom replies.

I start drawing bright red apples on Tom's tree, secretly wishing one of them would fall off and thunk the purple rabbit right on its fluffy white tail.

"It could use some birds too," Elizabeth butts in. She picks up an orange crayon and draws a bird on the branch I was planning to draw an apple on.

I frown. Shoot my ice pick eyes at her again. "*No* vacancy," I say, and draw a big red *X* over her dumb orange bird.

Elizabeth shoots a look back.

Tom chatters his teeth.

Alex steps to the front of the room and starts showing everyone examples of pinecone critters she's made. A mouse with felt ears and a yarn tail. A bird with feathery wings. A hedgehog with toothpick prickles and googly eyes. "Let your imaginations go wild," she says. "Literally! Make any kind of critters you want!"

Tom picks up a pinecone and studies it from every angle. "I'm thinking . . . fox," he says. "How about you two?"

I don't answer.

Neither does Elizabeth.

She's too busy drawing birds. I'm too busy drawing apples over them.

Then, just like that, she jumps up and clomps over to the supply shelf in her clunky cowboy boots. She takes a piece of paper from the *Help yourself!* box, clomps back, sits down, picks up the orange crayon, and starts drawing.

She keeps her arm crooked around the paper like she doesn't want me to cheat off her work. Dumb. Why would I need to copy *her* picture? She's not as good of a drawer as me.

I stretch my neck, looking.

She crooks her arm harder.

Dumber.

A minute later, she folds the paper like a card, flipping it over so fast there's no way I can see what she drew. Not that I care. Then she picks up a pinecone.

"I'm going to make a dog," she tells Tom.

Tom nods, gluing red felt ears to his pinecone. "The fox and the hound. Cool!"

He gives Elizabeth a friendly smile.

She gives him one back.

I pull a spike off my pinecone.

Loud laughter comes from the other table.

We all look.

Nat holds up a squashed pinecone. Red paint drips from its crushed spikes. Two googly eyes barely hang on.

"What *is* it?" Tom asks.

Nat does a sly grin. "Roadkill," she replies.

Emillie cracks up.

So does Brooke.

Stacey just smiles.

Chapter
10

"Our first Quiet Time," Meeka says when we get back to Chickadee after lunch. "We should commemorate the occasion."

She clicks a few pictures while we climb onto our bunks. We're supposed to relax and read and write letters until it's time to go to the beach. Sort of like rest time in kindergarten without the napping mats.

But I'm not tired. And I forgot to bring a book to read even though it was on my camp list. I have my sketchbook, but I don't feel like drawing. I did enough art at the crafts cottage this morning.

I glance at the pinecone critters that are sitting on the little table under my window. Stacey's cat. Elizabeth's dog. My monkey. Brooke's roadkill. She copied Nat's design.

But it's not the pinecone critters that keep catching my eye.

It's a card that Brooke insisted we prop up for everyone to see because she was the inspiration for it. The one Elizabeth made at the crafts cottage and kept hidden from me. A bright orange bird is on the cover, singing a bright orange song:

Tweet! Tweet!
Orange you glad to hear from me?!

After crafts, I saw Elizabeth show the card to Tom. Then I heard her say that she's going to mail it to her parents as soon as she writes a letter inside. That must be what she's doing now. I can hear her pencil scritch-scratching below me.

I pull George partway out of my sleeping bag so I know he can hear me thinking to him. *She's been away from her family for* one day, *George, and already she's sending them a card* and *a letter. She was away from me for a* whole year *and I didn't get one scribble.*

I hear someone laugh and glance across the room. Randi is reading a book. It must be funny, because she laughs again and turns the page. Stacey and Brooke are whispering. Meeka and Jolene are passing notes. Jenna is writing a letter. I wonder what she's telling her family. That she's having a good time? That Elizabeth is here? That she's moving back?

I look at the orange bird again. Then I stuff George down and pull out my notepaper and a purple gel pen from under my pillow.

I think for a moment. Then *I* start writing.

> If you ask me, it's R–U–D–E rude to pretend your favorite color is orange just so Brooke will like you. Obviously it's blue or you wouldn't paint your room that color. Plus, blue has always been your favorite. Or did you leave behind your favorite color too when you moved away?
>
> Ida

I slip the note through the crack between my bunk and the wall. Then I tuck away my pen, flip onto my back, and do a satisfied smile. "There," I whisper to George. "She may have Brooke fooled, but she can't fool me."

Elizabeth's bed creaks below me.

More scritch-scratching.

A minute later, a note rises up from the crack.

I snatch it and read the words.

> I think it's R–U–D–E–R <u>ruder</u> to X out someone's bird.
>
> Liz

I frown. But before I can crumple up the note and shoot for the wastebasket, *another* note appears.

It waves like a little flag.

I snatch it too.

> P.S. Blue is still my best color. Orange is my extra best.
>
> Not because of Brooke.
>
> Because of me.
>
> Things change, you know.
>
> Liz

I squeeze my fist around the note.

Take out another piece of paper.

Dig out my most unfavorite gel pen. Scribble down the words.

> I hope your parents L-O-V-E love the card. Let me know if you need help addressing the envelope.
>
> I

I let the note fall through the crack.
Wait.
Snatch the next one up.

> **We learned how to address envelopes in third grade. Duh-member?**
>
> **L**

> Of course I remember. But I thought you must have been sick that day since you for sure didn't know how to address an envelope to me when you moved to Albuquerque.
>
> I

I drop the note through the crack just as Alex steps into the room. "Quiet Time is over,

116

girls. You can get dressed for the beach."

I wait until Elizabeth goes to the bathroom to change, then I slide down from my bunk.

"I'll swim with you right after Randi and I race Rusty and Joey around the raft," Jenna tells me. She holds up her beach towel so I can change behind it. "They challenged us after our team beat the pants off their team in kickball."

"Great," I mumble, putting on my blue two-piece. "Brooke already asked Stacey to be her swimming buddy. That means I'm stuck with *you know who*."

"Don't worry," Jenna says from the other side of the towel. "It won't take us long to beat the boys again."

I take the towel as Jenna slips behind it to change.

The bathroom door opens. Elizabeth steps out, dressed in *her* swimsuit. It's the first time I've seen it, since she didn't take the swim test yesterday.

Two-piece.

Bright blue.

Exactly like mine.

I do a gasp.

"What is it?" Jenna asks, peeking out from behind the towel.

"She's got the *same suit,*" I wheeze.

Elizabeth walks up to us. "I know, I saw yours yesterday before you ran away to find . . . what was it? Oh yeah, something you lost."

No words come out of me even though my jaw is practically touching my chest. Elizabeth does that smile again. "Imagine my surprise when I saw that your suit was blue. I mean, your best color is *pink*. It's *always* been pink."

Jenna steps out from behind the towel. "Ida had hers first," she tells Elizabeth. "Go change."

Elizabeth snorts. "Into what? My birthday suit?"

"Fine with me." I finally find my voice. "Anything's better than looking like twins."

Elizabeth's face pinches. "If you want to wear *your* birthday suit, go ahead," she replies. "I'm wearing *this*." Then she does a sassy turn, sets her goofy glasses next to her orange bird, and picks up a lumpy beach bag.

I shove the towel back into Jenna's hands and

stomp over to Randi. "I need to borrow a T-shirt," I tell her, loud enough for Elizabeth to hear. "Something in an extra-large."

"Sure thing," Randi replies. She digs through her bag and pulls out a crumpled shirt. "This one is extra-*extra*-large."

Randi holds up the biggest, reddest T-shirt I've ever seen. *Peterson Plumbing* is printed on the front. So is a smiling toilet.

Randi grins. "Compliments of my dad."

I blink at the T-shirt. Do I want to wear a ginormous smiling toilet in public? No. But do I want to match Elizabeth Evans? Double no.

Sometimes you have to choose between the things you *don't* want the most.

I grab the shirt and slip it on over my suit.

The sleeves hang past my elbows.

The toilet touches my knees.

I hear snickering and look at Elizabeth. She bites back a smile.

"You're joking, right?" Brooke says, giving me the once-over. "You're not actually going to wear that thing to the beach."

I sigh. "That's my plan."

Brooke sniffs. "Then *my* plan is to swim as far away from you as possible."

She slips on her buggy sunglasses, takes Stacey's hand, and heads out the door.

Click!

Meeka looks up from her camera. "Got it!" she says, smiling at me.

"Meeka!" I shout. "I don't want a picture of me wearing this!"

"But it's a memory," Meeka replies. "Our first day playing at the beach."

I snatch the camera from her and push the erase button. "There," I say as the picture bleeps off the screen. "Now it's an *un*memory."

Alex steps into the doorway, watching, as I jam the camera back at Meeka.

Meeka takes it, frowning. "That was mean."

"It was mean of you to take Ida's picture without her permission," Jenna puts in.

Meeka gives Jenna a frown too. Then she, Randi, and Jolene brush past Alex, shooting looks back at us as they head out the door.

"I'll get your towel from the line," Jenna tells me. "Meet outside."

Alex studies me and Elizabeth for a moment after Jenna leaves. "Is anything wrong?" she asks. "Everyone seems a little upset."

Elizabeth adjusts the beach bag on her shoulder. "Nothing's wrong with *me*," she replies.

Alex turns my way. "Ida?" she asks. "Everything okay?"

My face feels as red as my T-shirt. My eyes sting with tears. I feel bad about grabbing Meeka's camera. I don't like that she's mad at me. But it's not my fault. If Elizabeth hadn't shown up wearing the exact same swimsuit as me, none of this would have happened. In fact, everything would be perfect if she hadn't shown up at all.

I blink away the sting. "Everything is fine," I reply.

Then I head out the door.

Chapter
11

"Turn it inside out," Jenna says a few minutes later, when we get to the beach. The other girls are already halfway to the raft. "Then you won't match Liz*butt,* and no one will see the toilet."

I give Jenna a smile of relief. "That's a good idea," I say, slipping the T-shirt off and turning it inside out.

Jenna lifts her chin. "I'm an expert at good ideas."

Elizabeth comes up from behind us.

Jenna gives her a squint. "What do *you* want?"

Elizabeth sets down her beach bag and taps her chin. "French fries and a strawberry shake," she replies. "How about you?"

"Ha-ha," Jenna says. "I mean, what are you doing here? *We're* swimming together as soon as I win my race." She takes my hand.

"I know," Liz replies, reaching into her bag. "But I thought we could explore until you get back."

She pulls out a face mask. Bright green, with buggy frog eyes on top. The lens looks like the frog's wide-open mouth. She snugs it over her eyes. Then she pulls out a pair of matching green flippers.

Jenna shakes her head, giving Elizabeth the once-over. "There isn't a kiddie pool at camp. You look like my little sister."

Elizabeth slips the flippers on her feet. "How *is* Rachel?" she asks. "I always liked *her*."

Jenna squints again.

Elizabeth waddles to the edge of the water. "Want to go over by those weeds?" she asks me, pointing to the far side of the shallow end. "If we stand still for a minute, fish will swim right up to us. Maybe even nibble our ankles!"

I just stare at her frog face mask. At her green flippers. At her blue two-piece that would be just as cute as mine, if *mine* wasn't hidden under a giant T-shirt.

How can she think that I would want to explore with her? How can she pretend that everything is the same between us? Wasn't she paying attention back at the cabin? Didn't she read my notes?

"C'mon, Jenna!" Randi hollers from the rope. Rusty and Joey are already by the raft, squirting water through their teeth and doing their best to bug Brooke while she tries to impress Nat and Emillie.

Jenna turns to me. "I'll be right back," she says. "We'll get my squishy ball and play catch."

"Sounds like fun!" Elizabeth chimes in.

Jenna glares at Elizabeth. "I was talking to Ida. Catch is no fun with *three.*"

"We could play Marco Polo," Elizabeth offers. "You need at least three for that."

Jenna gives me a *doesn't-this-girl-ever-give-up?* look.

"I know a game three can play," I say, turning to Elizabeth.

Elizabeth's eyes brighten behind her frog face mask. "What?" she asks.

I cross my arms. "Keep-away."

ඏ

"Trust me, you guys will *love* Nat and Emillie once you get to know them," Brooke says, later, after swimming. We're all sitting at a picnic table by the beach, eating sundaes the counselors are serving.

"I still don't think you should have told them about our snacks," Stacey grumbles. She scoops up a spoonful of ice cream.

Randi's spoon stops halfway to her mouth. "You *told* them?"

"Of course I told them," Brooke replies. "They're my friends. We're planning a party at their *secret* hideout! I'm calling it the *Sneak-n-Sweets, All You Can Eat Meet and Greet!* Isn't that completely imaginative?! They're even going to make us honorary *Hawks*!"

Brooke digs into her sundae.

Jenna lets out a steamy breath, like she's eating hot soup instead of ice cream. "I know plenty of secret spots. We don't need *Rat* and *Enemmie* to show us theirs."

Brooke licks sprinkles off her spoon. "You're just jealous because they like me best. Don't come if you don't want to."

"They're not your friends, Brooke," Jenna says back. "If you can't see that, then you need glasses worse than Liz*butt*."

Elizabeth shoots a look at Jenna. "My name is *Li—*"

"Where's the hideout?" I jump in.

Brooke shrugs. "Somewhere in the woods."

Meeka looks up from her sundae. "But that's where the Meadowlark Monster lives."

"Yeah, what if the monster eats *us* before we eat the candy?" Randi asks.

"Oh, *puhlease,*" Brooke says. "There are eight of us. *Ten* counting Nat and Emillie. *One* monster doesn't stand a chance."

Meeka thinks this through. "Maybe we could take his picture and then run away fast."

"I promise not to delete that one," I say to Meeka.

She gives me a smile.

"They'd put it on display for sure," Stacey says. "Right next to the one of us winning the Silver Paddle!"

"We might even get on the news!" Randi adds. *"Campers Conquer Meadowlark Monster!"*

Everyone giggles and nods.

"Works for me," Brooke says. "We'll sneak out with Nat and Emillie, and if that dumb monster comes around, we'll take his picture and get famous. Who's in?"

Randi raises her hand. "Me!"

Stacey, Meeka, and Jolene raise their hands too.

"There's something fishy about this plan," Jenna says, "but you would be lost without me. I'm in."

Brooke looks at me. "And you, Ida? Are you sneaking out with us?"

My stomach tightens. I don't want to get caught sneaking out, but I don't want to get left out either.

"In," I say.

Brooke turns to Elizabeth. "How about you?"

Elizabeth doesn't answer right away. She's busy sculpting her sundae into an ice cream castle. She got lots of practice making castles at the beach while me and Jenna played catch, and hunted for pretty rocks and snail shells, and buried them like treasure in the sand. Then we went to the crafts cottage and drew treasure maps. We forgot to invite Elizabeth along, accidentally on purpose.

Elizabeth looks up from her ice cream castle, her eyes bright with an idea. "You'll need someone to stay behind and be the lookout, won't you?"

"Ooo . . ." Brooke says. "That's clever. I wonder why I didn't think of it."

Randi nods. "It'll be just like a spy movie. Liz can do bird calls to warn us if someone is coming."

"That won't work," Jenna cuts in. "Birds aren't out at night."

"Owls are." Elizabeth cups her hands around her mouth and tips up her chin, just like the boys did when they sang *Figaro* this morning. "Who-who-whooo!" she calls to the gathering clouds.

"Perfect!" Stacey says. "You sound just like an owl!"

Jenna huffs. "I've heard better."

"It's settled then," Brooke says. "Liz will stay by Chickadee. If anyone comes poking around, she'll *hoot* and we'll *scoot*!"

"When do we sneak out?" Jolene asks. "Tonight?"

Brooke shakes her head. "Nat and Emillie have some very important texting to do tonight.

And tomorrow night is Hawk cabin's campout. So we'll have to wait until Wednesday. But that's okay because it will give me time to plan out all the details. When we'll leave . . . where we'll meet . . . what we'll wear . . . everything!"

"We should wear fake mustaches and carry the candy in a briefcase," Randi puts in. "That's how spies do it."

"I am *not* wearing a mustache," Brooke replies. "And where are we going to get a briefcase?"

"Mustaches? Candy? A bricfcasc?" Rusty and the other boys walk up to us. "What's going on?"

"None of your business," Brooke says, pulling her sundae away from Joey as he reaches for it.

"Aw, c'mon," Rusty says, squishing in. "What are you guys cooking up?"

"My lips are sealed." Brooke pinches her mouth like a prune.

"Then you won't be needing this." Joey swipes Brooke's sundae and takes a lick.

All the boys snicker.

Brooke snarls. "I wouldn't tell you apes our plan in a million *eons.*"

"That's a long time," Tom says.

Elizabeth nods. "Indefinitely long."

Quinn snorts. "And not one moment more."

They do a three-way smile.

I frown. "We're sneaking out," I say.

Quinn turns from Elizabeth to me. "Seriously?"

I nod, happy to take the attention away from her.

"You weren't supposed to tell, Ida," Brooke snaps.

I eat the cherry off my sundae. "Oops."

The boys nudge in.

"We need details," Tom says.

Rusty nods. "Spill it, Brooke."

Brooke clamps her mouth shut again. But her lips squirm, trying to let the words out. Brooke loves an audience. And right now, eleven pairs of eyes are on her.

"Fine," she finally blurts. "But you boys have to *swear* not to tell anyone. The future of my friendships depends upon it."

"Cross my heart and hope you die," Rusty says, flicking a freckled finger across his chest.

The other boys flick their fingers too.

Before I can even finish scraping the last of my hot fudge out of my sundae bowl, the whole story gushes out of Brooke like this is Yellowstone National Park and she's Old Faithful.

"Plus, if we see the monster, we're going to take his picture and get famous!" Meeka adds.

Joey snorts. "One look at the Meadowlark Monster and you *girls* will be crying for your *mommies*!"

Stacey straightens up. "Girls are way braver than boys."

Rusty slaps the picnic table, laughing. "Good one, Stacey," he says. "Got any more?"

As soon as we finish our sundaes, Alex takes us boating. Me, Stacey, Brooke, Randi, and Elizabeth in one rowboat. Meeka, Jolene, Jenna, and Alex in the other. We don't get back until suppertime because rowboats don't always go in the direction you want them to. Especially when gray clouds are stirring up the wind.

Then, after supper, Alex takes us on a nature hike. When we get to the clearing where the trust fall platform is, she makes us sit on the ground and close our eyes and listen to the sound of evening settling in.

At first, evening doesn't sound like it's settling in at all. It sounds like it's having a slumber party. And all the chipmunks and birds and insects are invited. Chattering. Chirping. Buzzing.

But if you make yourself sit still and silent long enough, all the noisy sounds soften until you swear you can hear the trees yawning and the grass bending and the flower petals folding. It makes you want to open your eyes and look around to see if the animals are sneaking out from behind the trees to gather near you, like fish circling your ankles.

But when I take a peek, I don't see any animals. I only see Elizabeth Evans, peeking back at me.

I close my eyes again.

"Any takers on the trust fall tonight?" Alex asks, breaking the silence a few minutes later.

Meeka and Jolene say, "Okay."

I say, "No."

Elizabeth says, "No thanks."

Brooke says, "No way."

౭౦౨

I lie awake after Alex gets done reading more about the girl who lives with wolves, listening to raindrops play patty-cake on the roof, and thinking about all the stuff that happened today. Camp stuff. Friendship stuff too.

How Randi and Elizabeth kept splashing everyone with their oars on our boat ride, and how Meeka and Jolene practically fell into the lake, trying to splash them back. How Brooke promised to reward Elizabeth with an extra sucker at the sneak-out because she came up with the clever idea of carrying the candy in a pillowcase. How we sang goofy songs at the campfire. How Stacey's and Elizabeth's marshmallows plopped into the flames at the exact same time, and how they hung on to each other, trying to hold in their giggles, while Randi used a stick to dub them the Knights of the Burnt Marshmallows.

I roll toward the wall and pull George under my chin.

"Everyone likes her," I whisper to him. "Except Jenna and me."

George shifts in my arms, like he can't decide whose side he's on.

I hear scritch-scratching below me. Maybe Elizabeth's mosquito bites are itching her too.

Scritch . . . scritch . . . scratch . . .

She must have a lot of them, because the sound goes on for a long time.

When it finally stops, her bed creaks.

A papery shadow rises up from the crack by the wall.

I shine my flashlight on it and see lots of words.

Ida,

I know you're mad at me for not sending you any letters. I knew it before I even moved back. But I thought once you saw me again, you'd be so happy you'd forget about being mad. And then I wouldn't have to explain why I did what I did. It was D-U-M-B dumb of me to think that way.

I know you have new friends now. I'm glad you do. Really. It's okay if you don't want to be friends with me. I just wish we didn't have to be enemies.

Liz

I read the note again.

I let George read it too.

When he's done, I wait for him to say something. But, like always, he doesn't say a word.

So I stick the note under my pillow and turn off my flashlight.

George snuggles in.

Thunder rumbles in the distance.

I lie awake for a long time.

Chapter
12

We're supposed to be cleaning our cabin on Tuesday morning while Alex is at her staff meeting, but we voted 7–1 to give ourselves the morning off. We're all tired and a little cranky from the storm that rolled through last night. Thunder sounds a lot scarier when you're away from home. Even if you are with mostly friends.

Instead, we're sitting on our bunks, eating the candy Brooke rationed out for today. One sucker each. Green or red because those are her least favorite colors. She's saving all the rest of the candy for our sneak-out tomorrow night.

I look across the room at Stacey. She's lying on her bunk, twirling a red sucker in her mouth, looking at a magazine and pretending to listen to Brooke babble on and on about Nat and Emillie.

"Hey, Stacey," I say, pulling the green sucker out of my mouth.

Stacey looks over.

I flick my green tongue in and out like I'm a frog catching flies. Then I smile and wait for her to laugh.

But she doesn't. She just shifts the sucker in her mouth and turns the page in her magazine.

I sigh. She's mad because of what I did to Elizabeth at breakfast this morning. When Elizabeth asked Jolene to please pass the last cinnamon roll, I snatched it first and took a bite. I also accidentally on purpose knocked over Elizabeth's cup, sopping her in orange juice. Instead of apologizing, I fake said, "I'm *soooo* sorry."

Stacey saw it all. I tried to link up with her on the way back to the cabin after breakfast, but she pulled away from me like my arm was electrified or something.

Stacey doesn't know about the note I got from Elizabeth last night. I'd show it to her if she'd give me a chance. Then she'd understand why I'm being a tiny bit mean.

Elizabeth knew I'd be mad at her for never writing to me. Still, she made it sound like I'm supposed to feel sorry for her. But I was just as sad, and I mailed *lots* of letters. Why couldn't she?

I should show the note to Jenna. She's good at organizing mixed-up stuff. And right now, I'm feeling very mixed up inside.

But Jenna would say the same thing whether she reads the note or not. She would tell me I don't need Elizabeth Evans as long as I have her around. Which is true. I have new friends. I don't need an old one. So why am I worried about it?

Because of Stacey.

She's not as organized as Jenna—seriously, you should see her room. Still, if you were at her house and asked to borrow her magenta hair band—the one with the silky white flower—she would say "Help yourself" and you would say "I would, if I had X-ray vision," and then she would scan around her messy room for a minute and, one second later, reach into that mess and pull the magenta hair band out.

Stacey can see things that other people can't. Plus, she knows how it feels to move away. I think that's why she wants me to give Elizabeth another chance.

But I did give Elizabeth chances.

Tons.

She let them all slip away.

I don't want a friend who doesn't even try.

I finish my sucker and then reach under my pillow for my sketchbook. I'm taking it with me to morning activities so Alex can see it. Me and Jenna are going to walk with her to the crafts cottage.

But as I pull out my sketchbook, Elizabeth's note from last night comes with it. I pick it up and read it again. *What does she mean . . . "I wouldn't have to explain why I did what I did"? What did she do, besides not write to me?*

"Garbage," someone says.

I look up.

Elizabeth is standing next to my bunk. She's wearing a different outfit now. One that doesn't smell like orange juice.

"Huh?" I say.

"Garbage," she says again, holding out her hand. "Sucker wrappers and sticks? I'm collecting them before Alex gets back. General Jenna's orders."

"Oh," I say, giving her mine.

"Thank you *soooo* much," she replies. Then she glances at the note in my hand. "Catching up on your reading?" She blinks, all innocent, behind her glasses.

I squint. And crumple the note. "No," I say, plunking it into her hand. "This is garbage too."

Elizabeth's eyes flash. She sucks in a sharp breath, like she's getting ready to shoot poisoned words at me. But then she hesitates and lets the breath out again.

She turns around, clomps to Brooke's backpack, and stuffs all the garbage away.

"These are great drawings, Ida," Alex says, turning pages in my sketchbook as we walk with Jenna to the crafts cottage a little later. "You're a good artist!"

"Told you so," Jenna tells her. She looks at me. "Go on, Ida. Give Alex the tour."

I smile and turn to a new page, happy to be away from Stacey's frowns and Elizabeth's poison glances. "That's my mom and dad," I say, pausing on a picture of a woman and a man with very white teeth. I even drew sparkles. Plus, musical notes in the air. "My dad is an orthodontist," I explain, "and my mom teaches piano."

"They look nice," Alex says.

"They are," I reply, and flip to a new picture. But when I see which one it is, I quickly flip past it. "And that's my house," I say, pointing at the next page. "See the window? That's my room." I flip again. "This is my school. And that's my whole class. See the guy with the ponytail? He's our teacher, Mr. Crow."

"*Was* our teacher," Jenna corrects me. "We'll be in fifth grade now."

"Wait," Alex says, flipping back. "You missed one." She stops at the picture I skipped. "That looks like you, but who's the other girl?"

Jenna glances over. Does a sniff. "No one," she says.

"She must be someone to Ida," Alex replies. "Look at the cool border she drew around her!"

I don't look at the picture. I don't need to. I have it memorized. Two girls with their arms wrapped around each other's shoulders. Matching hair. Matching friendship bracelets. One with a bandage on her chin.

"The other girl is Elizabeth," I mumble. "*Liz,* I mean. She didn't have glasses back then. Or short hair. We were"—I glance at Jenna—"*she* was . . . in our class. But then she moved away."

Alex nods. "You must be excited that she's moving back!"

"Thrilled," Jenna puts in.

"What happened to her chin?" Alex asks, pointing to the bandage I drew on Elizabeth's face.

"Rollerblade accident," I reply. "We sort of collided. She got a cut on her chin. I got a bruise on my butt that was shaped like a lightning bolt. It would have been a great show-and-tell if I could have shown anyone."

Alex chuckles. "You two have been through a lot together, huh?"

I shrug.

Jenna takes my hand.

"Please pass the cheese *turds*."

Joey points to a plastic bag that's lying next to me, filled with little lumps of yellow cheese. You're supposed to call the lumps cheese *curds,* but the boys never do.

I throw the bag at Joey. Not that I really need to. He's sitting three butt scoots away. The other boys aren't much farther behind.

Normally, I don't sit within scooting distance of them unless a teacher makes me. But, normally, I don't eat lunch with them on a raft. Alex and Connor rowed all of us out here after morning activities, plus our food. Mini bagels. Peanut butter. Grapes. Cheese curds. Punch. It's all spread out like a picnic in the middle of the raft. We make a sloppy circle around it.

"Sheesh, Ida," Joey says, nabbing the bag before it tumbles into the lake. "Work on your throw. No one likes soggy *turds*!"

The boys do a snort quartet.

Some of the girls glance over. I try to catch Stacey's eye, but she looks away before I can. I've been trying to catch it since me and Jenna met up with her and the other girls after our morning activities.

But Stacey isn't interested in having an eye conversation with me. She isn't interested in having a mouth one either.

I nibble a mini bagel and try not to look at Elizabeth. But my eyes keep darting to her anyway.

She's pulling off her clunky cowboy boots.

Now she's peeling off her mismatched socks.

Now she's dangling her feet in the water.

Picking up a grape.

Peeling off the skin.

I twitch a tiny smile because we always used to peel our grapes. Then we'd pretend they were slippery eyeballs and dare each other to eat them. Then we would. Which was gross. But also fun.

I take another nibble and glance again.

Stacey has scooted in next to her now. She starts peeling grapes too.

Talking with Elizabeth.

Laughing.

Squealing and gobbling down eyeballs together.

"Ignore them. She's just trying to punish you."

I look over and see Jenna rearranging herself closer to me.

"Huh?" I say.

"Stacey's mad because you're not being all huggy-huggy with Liz, right?" Jenna asks in a low voice.

I nod.

"So now Stacey's pretending to be friends with her just to make you mad. Don't give in and she'll give up. You and Stacey will be friends again. Nothing changes."

I pick up my punch cup and take a sip.

"Am I right?" Jenna asks, reaching for one of my grapes and popping it into her mouth. She looks like she already knows the answer is *yes*.

"You're one part right," I reply.

Jenna stops chewing. "*One* part?"

I nod. "And *two* parts wrong."

Jenna frowns.

"You're right about Stacey being mad at me," I explain. "But you're wrong about her fake friending Elizabeth. Stacey never fakes friendship. She's friending Elizabeth for real."

Jenna grabs another grape and starts chewing again. "That's only *one* wrong."

"You're also wrong about things not changing," I continue. "Because they already have. Elizabeth is back even though I don't want her to be. The other girls are her friends now. And no matter what, friendship changes things. Not always in the way you want."

Jenna sniffs. "Very touching," she says. "But *you're* wrong about something too."

"What?" I ask.

Jenna stands up and pops my last grape into her mouth. "You *do* want her back." She checks her watch and turns to Alex and Connor. "Lunch-time is over."

We clean up the raft and then row back to shore. I spend the rest of Tuesday keeping as far away from Elizabeth Evans as possible, just to prove that Jenna is wrong again.

Chapter

13

The next morning Brooke glances up from stuffing candy into her pillowcase. It's Wednesday, the day of our sneak-out. She zeros in on Jenna. "Who's next on the trust fall schedule?"

Jenna looks up from refolding the clothes in her suitcase. She's making us clean Chickadee extra-good today, since we outvoted her yesterday and didn't clean up at all. She even got Stacey to put a pair of socks on her hands and pick dead flies off the windowsills. Plus, she sent Randi, Meeka, and Jolene outside with brooms to sweep cobwebs from the cabin walls. "Technically, *you,* since you skipped your turn."

"I'm planning the whole sneak-out," Brooke replies, adding a package of gum and a fistful of suckers to the pillowcase. "I'm not falling too."

"Then Ida and Liz*butt* are tied for next tallest," Jenna tells her.

Elizabeth stops rearranging the pinecone critters. She scowls at Jenna. "I've told you a million times. My name is *Liz.*"

Jenna rolls her eyes. "*Butt*ever."

"One of you has to fall as soon as possible," Brooke says to me and Elizabeth. "We need Alex to take us to the platform before it gets dark."

"So the monster won't get us?" Randi asks, coming inside again with Meeka and Jolene.

Brooke huffs. "I don't care about that silly monster. All I care about is my plan." She sets the pillowcase aside and scoots to the edge of her bunk, like she doesn't want us to miss one word. "Jenna, you should be writing this down."

Jenna grumbles and scoots her suitcase away. She isn't in favor of Brooke's sneak-out plan, but she *is* in favor of being organized. She climbs onto her bunk and pulls out her clipboard and a pen. "Go," she says to Brooke.

Brooke clears her throat and begins again. "We'll leave Chickadee at the *beep* of midnight. Jenna will set the alarm on her watch."

Jenna makes a note on her clipboard.

"Everyone wear regular clothes to bed so we can leave quietly without waking up Alex. *Dark* clothes. And *no* flashlights, or someone might see them shining through the trees. Liz will keep watch by the cabin. The rest of us will go to the trust fall platform. Nat and Emillie are meeting us there."

"Why can't they just take us straight to the hideout?" I ask.

"Because that's not how it's done," Brooke explains. "First, you meet up at a secret spot. Then, you go on a journey. Finally, you arrive at your destination." She counts off each step on her fingers.

Elizabeth nods. Then she looks at me. "It's called *drama,* Ida."

I give her a squint. "You're not even going with us. I call that *chicken.*"

I hear a muffled laugh and look over at Jenna. She gives me a thumbs-up.

Then I look at Stacey.

She gives me a frown.

"But if we don't bring flashlights," Meeka says,

brushing cobwebs off her shirt, "we'll never find the platform."

"Already thought of that," Brooke replies. "All we have to do is mark the trees with glow-in-the-dark paint! I saw some in the crafts cottage. We'll be just like Hansel and Gretel, following a trail of bread crumbs!"

"But the birds *ate* their bread crumbs," Jolene points out.

Randi nods. "And a witch almost ate *them*." She mounts her broom and does a wicked cackle.

"That's why *my* plan is better," Brooke says. "Birds don't eat paint." Her eyes hopscotch from girl to girl. "Someone has to go to Alex's craft this morning and get it. The glow-in-the-dark paint, I mean. Any volunteers?"

"Not me," Randi says, circling the room on her broomstick. "I'm playing kickball."

Jenna nods in agreement.

So does Stacey.

"Meeka and I signed up for bird watching," Jolene says.

"So did I," Elizabeth puts in. "Tom too."

"I'm going on a nature hike with Nat and

Emillie," Brooke says. Then she barks a laugh. "*Not!* Actually, we're going to hide in Hawk and text their friends!"

She throws me a look. "That means you have to get the paint, Ida. Thank you for volunteering."

"But I didn't—"

"It's next to the glitter," Brooke cuts in. "You can't miss it."

"But I don't want to—"

"Wear something with big pockets so you can get a lot."

I narrow my eyes. "I don't think the trees want to get painted, Brooke. And I don't want to steal for you."

Someone clucks like a chicken. I whip a look at Elizabeth.

Brooke does an impatient sigh. "It's not stealing if we don't take it away from camp. And since when do trees care about how they look? They have branches, not brains. Besides, you're not doing it for *me*. You're doing it for all of us. Your *friends*. Remember?"

"Friends don't make each other do things they don't want to do," Stacey puts in.

I blink, surprised she's defending me.

Elizabeth nods and steps in next to Stacey. "You're not the boss of us, Brooke. Not even Ida."

I frown. What does she mean, *not* even *Ida? I'm more a part of the group than she is.*

Brooke snorts. "I'm not *making* Ida get the paint. I'm *asking* her to get it. *Friends* help each other."

Elizabeth links arms with Stacey. "That's what we're doing. Helping Ida."

My stomach burns like I put hot sauce on my pancakes this morning instead of maple syrup. "Brooke isn't bossing me. And I don't need *your* help." I step toward Elizabeth and punch my fists into my hips. "So *butt out, Lizbutt.*"

A gasp circles the room. It's the only time I've ever called anyone a name outside of my own head. I swallow hard and turn my face to agate.

Elizabeth steps toward me and narrows her eyes. "If you want me to butt out, then I'll butt out . . . I-*duh.*" She gives my shoulder a jab.

More gasps.

My knees turn into springs.

I pounce.

Elizabeth hits the floor.

Her glasses fly.

I fall on top of her.

"Stop it, Ida!" Stacey shouts. "You're acting crazy!" She pulls me off of Elizabeth.

I scramble to my feet and push Stacey away, tears brimming in my eyes. "She's the one who's crazy!" I shout. I glare at Elizabeth. She's still sprawled on the floor, her eyes bright with tears too and her face as red as her cowboy boots. "You can't come back here and act like everything is fine. Stuff *isn't* fine. You moved away and never wrote to me. Do you know how sad that made me? It felt like my heart broke. I wish you never came back!"

Tears flood my eyes. All the girls' faces swim around me. Wide-eyed. Mouths open. Like they're looking at a monster.

Elizabeth gets up and stands boot to sneaker with me.

"Do you know how sad it made *me* to move? It felt like my *stomach* broke. It hurt so bad I had to go see a *doctor*. She made me write about the hurt and mail it all away. I even had to send letters to my *dog,* Champ. Stupid, huh? But when I tried to send letters to you, my stomach hurt more than ever. Because it reminded me that I missed *you* more than anyone."

Tears stream down her cheeks, but she doesn't wipe them away. "I wrote lots of letters to you. *Tons.* They're all inside my valentine volcano. I stuffed them in until the lava cork wouldn't stay stuck. Then I stopped writing. Because I figured you had new friends by then and didn't need an old friend like me. I was hoping I was wrong, but now I know it's true."

Elizabeth turns away, crying harder. Stacey puts an arm around her.

Jenna hops down from her bunk and puts an arm around me.

Brooke does a big sigh. "Look, I hate to interrupt the dramarama, but Alex will be back any second. And I. Need. *Paint.*" She looks at me. "Pull yourself together, Ida."

"Sheesh, Brooke," Randi says. "Some things are more important than your stupid plan."

Brooke glares at Randi. "My plan is not stup—"

The cabin door opens. Brooke quickly pulls her sleeping bag over the candy.

"Hi!" Alex says, stepping into the room. "I'm ba—"

She stops short, taking in the scene. Stacey holding Elizabeth. Jenna holding me. Both of us crying.

Alex rushes up to us. "What happened?"

"It's the funniest thing." Brooke hops down from her bunk and picks up Elizabeth's glasses. "Ida fell off her bunk. *Thunk!* She landed right on top of poor Liz."

Brooke hands the glasses back to Elizabeth. "No harm done, though. Her lenses didn't even get scratched."

Alex checks us up and down. "Does anything hurt?"

"No," Elizabeth says, straightening her glasses and glancing at me. "Nothing hurts."

I rub my eyes, sniffling. "Same here."

Stacey gives me a squint. "Don't you want to tell Liz you're sorry for *falling* on her?"

"Why should she?" Jenna cuts in. "Like Brooke said, it was an accident."

Brooke pins on a cheerful smile. "All's well that ends well!" She looks at Alex again. "Ida was just saying how much she wants to do crafts this morning."

Brooke turns to me. "Isn't that right, Ida?"

I pin on a smile too.

"Great, if you feel up to it," Alex says to me, still looking concerned. "We can walk over together."

"And Liz is just *dying* to do the trust fall," Brooke continues. "Aren't you, Liz *dear*?"

"Can't wait," Elizabeth mumbles.

Alex gives her a smile. "We'll go after lunch."

Brooke grins.

I hurry to the bathroom and splash cold water on my face while the other girls change into sneakers and rub on sunscreen and head out to play kickball and watch birds and go on a fake hike through nature. I pat my face dry and take my time smoothing down my damp bangs. I'm in no hurry to see that look on Stacey's face again. The one she had when I didn't apologize. Like I let *her* down.

I wait until I hear the screen door snap shut

for the last time. Then I peek out. And hurry to my bunk.

I reach around under my sleeping bag, searching for my notepaper and a pen, but I find a monkey first.

George grunts and comes up for air.

"Did you hear what happened?" I ask him.

George gives me a *Duh* look. Sock monkeys have excellent hearing.

"The girls think I'm a monster," I continue. "Stacey, mostly, because I didn't apologize. But what about Elizabeth? You heard her, George. She didn't say *sorry* once for never sending those letters."

George studies me as I search around for my notepaper. "I need to write one more note. Then things will be right again."

The cabin door creaks open. Jenna steps in. "Are you coming?"

I tuck George back inside my sleeping bag and turn around. "I thought you were going to kickball," I say to Jenna.

Jenna shrugs. "Change of plan. I'm sticking with you."

I walk over to her. "You're not mad?"

Jenna's forehead crinkles. "For what? Liz pushed you first. She got what she deserved." Jenna lifts her chin and flicks back a braid. "Time for Liz*butt* Evans to *move on*."

I do a half smile. I'm happy Jenna is on my side. But I know Stacey isn't. And she won't be, until I write that note.

"Just give me *one* second," I say.

Jenna sighs and checks her watch. "Okay, but hurry. I'll tell Alex you're on your way."

Jenna marches out.

I grab my notepaper and write as fast as I can.

I'm sorry for what happened. Please don't stay mad at me.

Ida

Then I walk over to Stacey's bunk.

And leave the note on her pillow.

Chapter

14

"Looks like Pete dropped off our mail while we were at lunch," Alex says, later, when we get back to Chickadee for Quiet Time. A stack of letters is sitting on her desk. She passes them around. Two for Meeka . . . three for Randi . . . one for Jenna . . . one for me. Everyone gets something.

Stacey takes her mail from Alex and brushes past me on the way to her bunk.

She hasn't had a chance to find my *Sorry* note yet because after morning activities we went straight to the dining hall for lunch. When she does read it, she can stop being mad and start talking to me again.

Brooke, on the other hand, *has* had a conversation with me. Several. Because I didn't take any glow-in-the-dark paint this morning.

I explained to her that we went straight to the beach, instead of the crafts cottage, and pressed our hands in the wet sand and hunted around for interesting rocks and shells and arranged them in the handprints and covered them with goopy plaster. And how that took a long time. Then I explained how we didn't even go to the crafts cottage while the plaster dried. We all just sat on the stone wall and sang the Camp Meadowlark theme song and counted mosquito bites and discussed lip gloss flavors and summer movies and who would win the Silver Paddle and whether or not a monster really lives in the woods.

But Brooke wasn't interested in hearing any of my excuses. She blamed me for messing up her perfect plan. And said she would hold me personally responsible if I didn't skip swimming and get that paint this afternoon. And that it was my fault she had to waste her sweetest smile on Alex when she pretty-please asked her to reschedule Elizabeth's trust fall for later in the day.

Elizabeth heard Brooke's whole bossy speech to me. But, this time, she didn't butt in.

I climb onto my bunk and start reading my mail.

Hi, Ida!

We hope you're having lots of fun at camp! Guess who we ran into the other day? Elizabeth's mom and dad! They told us you two are at camp together, and that their family is moving back to Purdee. You must be SO excited!

See you soon!

Love,

Mom & Dad

I stick the letter back inside its envelope. "They think I'm excited, George," I whisper to the lump inside my sleeping bag. "They think nothing changes too."

I hear a snort come from Jenna's bunk. She unfolds a piece of paper and holds it up for me to see.

A crayon drawing of a big green frog with a note underneath it in little-kid print.

Get me one!

Frum, Rachel

Jenna shakes her head. "She never gives up." Then she props the picture on her pillow and gets busy reading the letter that came with it.

The bunk below me creaks. I hear that scritch-scratch sound again. Elizabeth must be writing another letter home. That makes two so far, because I saw her mail the orange bird yesterday.

Maybe she's telling her parents about the shoving incident. Her dad is some kind of lawyer. He'll probably sue me. Or have me arrested. I wonder if they'll put me in prison. I hope they allow sock monkeys there.

The sound stops.

Her bunk creaks again.

A note rises up from the crack.

I shake my head, just like Jenna. *She never gives up either.*

I'm just about to take the note when someone clears her throat behind me.

I turn and see Stacey standing by my bunk. "I'm not the one you should be apologizing to," she says, crisp as burnt toast. Then she drops my *Sorry* note on my bunk, turns around, and walks away.

I glance at the crack again.

The note is still there.

My heart chugs as I read the words.

Don't go to the crafts cottage right away.
Meet me at the beach.
I have a plan.
                                    Liz

"It's all Jenna's fault," Elizabeth says to me and Jenna when we meet up with her at the beach. Randi, Meeka, and Jolene went for a boat ride. Stacey and Brooke are already on the raft with Nat and Emillie. Brooke is so busy jabbering, she hasn't noticed that I'm here instead of at the crafts cottage.

Jenna's face scrunches. "*Nothing* is my fault."

Elizabeth sighs. "I said that wrong. I just meant . . . *you* gave me my idea."

Jenna crosses her arms. "I never gave you anything. Ida, I told you this was a bad idea."

Elizabeth nods. "No, you did." She points at Jenna's hair. At the ladybug barrettes clipped above her braids.

Jenna reaches up and clips them tighter. "I'm not *giving* you my barrettes. They were a gift from Ida."

"I don't want them," Elizabeth replies. "But they made me think of a way to get glow-in-the-dark paint without taking it."

"We're going to paint Jenna's barrettes?" I ask, confused.

Elizabeth smiles. "No," she replies. "We're going to paint *rocks* to look like *ladybugs*. If we use the glow-in-the-dark paint to make their dots, it won't be stealing. It will be art!"

Jenna huffs. "How's that going to help us—"

"We'll drop the ladybugs in the woods," Elizabeth interrupts. "By day, they'll blend in. By night, they'll *glow*!"

My eyes brighten. "We won't have to paint the trees," I say, catching on. "The ladybugs will lead the way."

Elizabeth nods.

Jenna frowns. Shifts her jaw. Thinks things through.

But even Jenna Drews has to admit it's a good plan. A moment later, she unclips a ladybug from hcr hair. "We'll use this one for a model," she tells us. Then she punches her fists into her hips and scrutinizes the rocks on the beach. "Not much of a selection, but it will have to do."

She looks at us again. "You two get busy collecting rocks. I'll find Pete and get a bucket."

Jenna marches off toward the maintenance shack.

Me and Elizabeth look at each other. This is the first time we've been alone since the shoving incident. It's easier to ignore stuff like that when other people are around. We look away again.

I pick up a rock and pretend to be very interested in rubbing the sand off it. I glance at Elizabeth. She's busy rubbing sand off a rock too. I think about what Stacey told me. *I'm not the one you should be apologizing to.*

"About what happened," I say. "I'm—"

"I'm sorry," Elizabeth blurts before I can get out another word. She looks at me. "For fighting with you."

"I'm the one who's sorry for that," I reply.

Elizabeth shakes her head. "I shoved you first."

"I shoved you *harder*."

"Only because I never wrote to you. I'm so sorry, Ida. I never meant to hurt you."

"Well, you did write. You just need to work on your mailing skills."

We look away again.

"Do you still have it?"

"Have what?"

I look up. "The valentine volcano?"

Elizabeth nods. "I lost the lava cork when we moved back, but the volcano is in my new closet. All the letters are still inside."

I do a half smile. "Good. I'd like to read them sometime."

Elizabeth does a half smile back. "Come over whenever you want."

If Brooke Morgan were here right now, instead of out on the raft trying to impress Nat and Emillie, she would be rolling her eyes. And telling us that it's L-A-M *lame* for friends to be wearing the exact same swimsuits.

Lamer for them to be hugging each other on the beach.

But who cares what Brooke Morgan thinks.

ℰℒℴ

"Hey, look!" Rusty shouts as he and the other boys hop down from the stone wall after me and Liz start collecting rocks again. He points at our matching swimsuits. "Tweedledee and Tweedledum!"

Joey snorts. "*Dee* and *Dumb*. Good one!"

Quinn laughs.

I give him a squint.

Tom gives us the once-over. "I think they're more like *Yin* and *Yang*."

Joey does a puzzled frown. "Yin and Yang? When are they on? Saturdays?"

"It's not a show," Tom replies. "It's a Chinese symbol. Two tadpoles in a circle." He draws the symbol in the sand. "They represent balance. You can't have one without the other."

Joey studies Tom's drawing. Then he looks at the two of us again. "I like *Dee* and *Dumb* better."

Quinn bobs his head.

So annoying.

Rusty looks past us. Taps Joey's arm. "Watch out," he hollers. "Here comes Tweedle*dumber*!"

Jenna hops down from the stone wall, carrying a plastic pail.

She gives Rusty a squint. "Go jump in a lake."

Rusty brightens. "Good idea!"

He and the other boys take off for the water.

Jenna studies me and Liz. Our smiling faces. Our matching swimsuits. Our sandy hands, clasped together. "Why are you two just standing around?" she asks. "C'mon, we've got work to do."

We start dumping rocks into the pail. When it's full, we take off for the crafts cottage. Me, Jenna, and Liz.

Just like she promised, Alex brings us to the trust fall platform before supper. Of course we didn't mark the trees with glow-in-the-dark paint on the way here. And we won't mark them on the way back either.

Because of Liz's good idea.

When Alex saw our bucket of rocks earlier, she decided to make rock painting the craft of the day. While everyone else in the crafts cottage got busy painting their rocks to look like fish and turtles and caterpillars, me, Jenna, and Liz painted our rocks to look like ladybugs. A whole flock of them. With glow-in-the-dark dots on their wings.

Then we blew on them to make the paint dry

faster. And ran with them to Chickadee, dizzy from all that blowing, and changed into our regular clothes and showed the ladybugs to the other girls.

At first, Brooke shot laser eyes at us because "ladybugs are not part of my plan."

But then Liz reminded her about Hansel and Gretel. And how they followed a path of bright pebbles through the woods. And how that was very imaginative of them.

Brooke took time to think this information through. Then she switched off her laser eyes and started telling the other girls about her *new* plan involving glowing ladybugs.

We all listened and nodded while Brooke babbled on and on about it, even though we already knew all the details by heart. Because this plan stopped being Brooke's plan twenty ladybugs ago. It's *our* plan now.

"Your turn, Brooke," Jenna says as we gather by the trust fall platform. "Then Liz."

Brooke sniffs and flicks back her long, smooth hair. "I already told you. I'm not falling. Not in a million eons."

Jenna frowns. "It's a rule, Brooke. Everyone has to fall sometime."

"Nu-uh," Randi puts in. "Alex said only if we want to."

Alex nods. "That's true. No one can force you to trust your friends."

Brooke huffs. "I trust my friends. I just don't think they can catch me."

"I'll go," Liz says.

Liz climbs onto the platform in her bright red cowboy boots.

Jenna rolls her eyes. Mumbles something about the rodeo coming to town.

Liz peers down at me from her perch. "Looks like it's my turn to fall on *you*," she says.

"Fall away," I say back.

We trade grins.

I see Stacey watching us. She smiles too. "Apology accepted," she says, and gives my arm a squeeze.

Liz turns around, stands like a domino and, a moment later, we catch her when she falls.

"Hey, that was fun!" she says, looking up at us. "Can I go again?"

"No," Jenna says. "One fall per customer."

"It's fine if Liz wants to," Alex says as we set Liz on her feet. "Same for all of you. You can fall as many times as—"

"Oh my," Brooke cuts in. "Look at the time. We'll be late for supper. Chop, chop! Let's go!"

Brooke isn't really looking at the time because she still isn't wearing a watch. But that's the secret signal we agreed on. Time to put our sneak-out plan into action.

Meeka and Jolene go to work.

"Tell us what happens next in the story about the girl and the wolves," Jolene says, taking Alex's hand.

Meeka takes her other one. "Yeah, does she survive, or do the wolves let her down?"

They tug Alex toward our cabin while they talk.

Brooke corrals them from behind.

She glances over her shoulder at me.

I nod. Then I reach into my pockets and pull out some ladybugs.

Liz does the same.

So does Stacey.

And Randi.

They follow the others at a distance, dropping ladybugs as they go.

I look at Jenna. She's watching Liz clomp through the trees.

"Coming?" I ask her.

Jenna leans against the trust fall platform. When Liz is out of sight, she turns to me. "Are you going back to being best friends with her?" she asks.

I bite my lip. Fiddle with my ladybugs.

Am I?

Going back?

If I did go back to being her best friend, then I would have to pretend that nothing has changed.

But stuff *has* changed.

Not just the things you can see, like haircuts and glasses.

Inside stuff has changed too.

Like who we trust now.

And who we don't.

Who lets us down.

And who picks us up again.

I walk over to Jenna.

"I'm not going *back* to being her best friend," I say.

Jenna narrows her eyes suspiciously. "You're not?"

"Nope," I reply. "I'm going *ahead* to being her best friend."

Jenna sighs. Nods. "I thought so."

"What about you?" I ask. "Are you going to be friends with Liz too?"

Jenna flicks back a braid.

Reclips her barrettes.

"Maybe," she replies. "If she loses the boots."

I smile and sling my arm around her shoulders.

We walk together through the woods, letting the ladybugs fall.

Chapter

15

I pretend to go right to sleep as soon as Alex finishes reading our bedtime story later on Wednesday night, but really I'm not even close to sleeping. I've never been able to stay awake past midnight before. But I've never snuck out of a dark cabin and crept through spooky woods at night before either.

Stuff like that can boost your energy.

I know Liz is awake too because I can hear her shifting around below me.

I pull George up from the bottom of my sleeping bag.

"I wish you could come with me," I whisper to him. "But the woods are no place for a monkey."

George does a sigh of relief. He's not a big fan of nature.

I hug him close. "Don't worry about me, though. I'll be with my friends."

Beep! Beep! Bee—!

The muffled beeping stops. I look over at Jenna's bunk. She's reaching under her pillow and pulling out her watch. That's where she put it so Alex wouldn't hear it go off.

"Ready?" she whispers to me.

"For anything," I whisper back.

Sleeping bags rustle.

Shadowy shapes tiptoe across the floor.

Liz opens the back door slowly, so it won't creak, letting in the moonlight. The other girls step past her. Randi. Stacey. Jenna. Meeka and Jolene.

Brooke pulls the candy-stuffed pillowcase from her bunk and cuts past me. She hates being last in line.

But she stops when she gets to Liz. "Don't let me down, Liz*butt*," she whispers. But not in a mean way.

"Wouldn't think of it, *Brooklyn* Bridge," Liz replies.

They both do sassy grins.

Then Brooke fishes around inside the pillowcase. "Here's the extra sucker I promised you. Carrying the candy in a pillowcase is way more imaginative than a backpack."

"Thanks!" Liz says, taking the sucker from Brooke. "I forgot about that promise."

"I never forget," Brooke replies, slipping out the door.

Which is true. Brooke Morgan has an excellent memory. And she always keeps a promise. Unless she crosses her fingers first.

"Better hurry," Liz says to me, tucking the sucker into her hoodie pocket. "Randi told me she's wearing tape over her light-up sneakers. If Brooke gets too bossy about keeping quiet and staying out of sight—I mean, *when* she gets too bossy—Randi's going to rip off the tape and run in circles around her."

I snort a laugh. "Can't wait."

Liz nods. "Tell me all about it when you get back."

"Deal," I reply. "Plus, I'll save you some candy. More than just a sucker."

Liz smiles. Then she gives me the once-over. "You look lumpy."

I glance down at the bulge under my sweat-shirt. "It's not me. It's my monkey."

I reach underneath and pull George out.

Liz does a happy gasp. "George!" she whisper-cries. "I've missed you!"

"He's missed you too," I reply. "*Tons.* In fact, he wants to keep you company while I'm gone."

Liz takes George and hugs him tight. "Thanks," she says.

"You're welcome," I say back.

"Ida!" someone whispers loudly.

I look outside and see six shadowy girls waving at me from the edge of the woods.

I turn to Liz. "Good-bye."

She waves George's hand. "See you soon."

"There it is!" Randi shouts a few minutes later, when we enter a clearing in the woods. The trust fall platform stands guard in the moonlight.

"Shhh!" Brooke hisses at Randi. "How many times do I have to tell you to keep it down?"

Randi shoots a look at Brooke. "Once more should do it."

We hurry to the platform.

"Now what?" Meeka whispers.

"Now we wait for Nat and Emillie," Brooke replies.

"But what if the monster gets here fir—"

Branches snap and leaves rustle.

We turn and gawk at a nearby bush.

Nat steps out from behind it.

"Finally," she grumbles, swatting the air. "I'm getting eaten alive out here. Where's the candy?"

Brooke lifts the pillowcase excitedly. "Here!" she says. "Where's Emillie?"

"She's . . . around," Nat replies, glancing at the bush.

Nat walks over to Brooke and holds out her hand. "Give the candy to me. I'll take it from here."

Jenna steps in. Crosses her arms. Lifts her chin. "Take it *where*?" she asks.

"Shhh!" Brooke scolds again. "We're going someplace safe. A little farther in the woods." She holds the pillowcase out to Nat.

Meeka gulps and fumbles for the camera in her pocket. "W-w-will we see the monster?"

"Yeah . . . sure . . . whatever . . ." Nat replies, snatching the candy and glancing around distractedly. She steps closer to the edge of the clearing, pulls a flashlight from her pocket, and blinks it on and off a few times.

"What's she doing?" Stacey whispers to me.

I shrug. "Signaling?"

Meeka clutches my arm. "Who? The monster?" She lifts her camera and points it at the trees.

Flash!

"Meeka!" Brooke shouts. "I said *no* lights!"

"It was an accident!" Meeka cries. "My hand was shaking!"

"Put the camera *away!*" Brooke snarls.

"That's it," Randi grumbles. She reaches down and starts pulling the tape off her blinking shoes.

"Whooo . . . who-who!"

Randi looks up.

We all do.

"What was that?" Jolene asks.

"The monster!" Meeka squeaks.

"No," Jenna replies. "It's Liz. Someone's coming!"

Heavy footsteps clomp toward us.

"Quick!" Nat yells. "Run!"

Everyone takes off.

Running.

Screaming.

Blinking.

Except me.

I just stand there, frozen in my sneakers.

"Whooo . . . who-who!"

The sound is closer now. Liz must be looking for us. There's no time to run even if I could.

I look around wildly for a place to hide.

Dive for the trust fall platform.

Duck underneath.

Crumple into a ball.

Hope I blend in.

I sit there until the noise stops. Until all I can hear are frogs chirping and my heart pounding.

Then that bush starts shaking again. I swallow a scream.

A light glows behind the branches.

But it's not a glowing monster eye.

It's a flashlight.

Nat and Emillie step into the clearing.

"It worked?" Emillie asks, glancing around.

Nat lifts the candy-stuffed pillowcase. "Like a charm."

Emillie smiles. "Lucky for us *Babbling* Brooke

spilled the beans on their secret signal. I do an excellent owl. Let's get out of here before the little dorks figure out we tricked them."

They point their flashlight into the darkness and creep away.

I wait for a minute.

Then I follow the ladybugs back to Chickadee.

The other girls are huddled together in the moonlight when I get there.

"What do you mean you didn't hoot?" Brooke says to Liz as I hurry up to them. "I *heard* you. We all did."

"It wasn't me," Liz replies, clutching George to her chest. "I've been here the whole time."

"Maybe it was a real owl," Jolene offers.

"No, it wasn't," I say, out of breath. "It was Emillie. I saw her. With Nat. They took the candy and ran."

Brooke huffs. "Of course they did. They didn't want to get caught."

I shake my head. "I heard them talking, Brooke. They tricked us."

"I *knew* it," Jenna grumbles.

Randi snorts. "Bye-bye candy."

"I never liked those girls much," Jolene says.

"Me neither," Meeka adds.

"Admit it, Brooke," Stacey says. "They were trouble from the start."

Brooke scowls. "You're *wrong*. All of you. *They* didn't trick us. Liz*butt* did."

Liz's mouth drops open. She squeezes George until his eyes bulge. "I *told* you," she says, her voice as sharp as broken glass. "My name is *Liz*. And I didn't—"

A flashlight beam hopscotches through the trees. Footsteps approach.

"See?" Brooke cuts in. She points excitedly at the light. "There they are now!"

For one tiny second, I think it might be true. Maybe Nat and Emillie decided to come back. Friends can change. Even bad ones.

The light shines on our faces.

We squint and shade our eyes.

A shadowy figure approaches.

Big, like a bear.

And hairy.

"Good evening, Chickadees," Pete says, lowering his flashlight. "Out for a midnight stroll?"

Chapter

16

"They weren't tricking us," Brooke says, Thursday morning, as we clean up our cabin while Alex is at her staff meeting. It's the first chance we've had to talk about what happened last night after Pete caught us sneaking out. And after Alex gave us a lecture about following the rules, and made us pick up all the ladybugs, and told us we would have to weed the camp garden instead of going to morning activities today. "They're our friends."

"If that's true, how come our *friends* don't have to weed the garden?" Randi grumbles.

"Because we didn't tell on them," Brooke replies. "That proves we're good friends too."

Jenna looks up from sweeping. "They didn't care if we got into trouble, Brooke."

Stacey nods. "All they cared about was getting our candy."

Brooke scowls. "No they didn't. They weren't setting us up."

Jenna stops sweeping. "If that's true, then go ask them to give it back."

Brooke narrows her eyes at Jenna. Then she jumps down from her bunk. "Fine," she snips. "I will."

She marches out the door.

"This I gotta see," Randi says, dropping her broom and flying after Brooke.

We all do.

Out the door.

Down the steps.

Across the dewy grass to Hawk cabin.

"If you're selling Girl Scout cookies," Emillie says, a minute later, when Brooke bangs on the door, "we're not buying." She smiles sweetly through the screen, chewing a wad of gum. I bet I know where she got it.

"About last night," Brooke begins.

Emillie crosses her arms. Chews her cud. "What about it?"

"We got caught," Brooke says. "Did you?"

Nat pokes in. She studies us through the screen like we're bugs in a box. "Caught?" she says innocently. "Doing what?"

Brooke blinks. "Sneaking out. With *us*. With our *candy*." She stretches her neck, trying to see into the cabin. "Where is it, by the way?"

Nat and Emillie square their shoulders, blocking Brooke's view. They look at each other, do matching smiles, and then look at us again. "What candy?" they singsong together.

Brooke's jaw tightens. Her nostrils flare. "You . . . you took it," she says. "And then you told us we'd go to the hideout . . . and then there was a noise in the woods . . . and we ran . . . and . . ."

"Calm down, Brooke," Emillie cuts in. "You're *babbling* again. We don't know what you're talking about."

Nat twirls one of her curls. "Yeah, *Babs*. It was probably just a bad dream."

I frown. "Uh-huh, and you two had the starring roles."

Liz nods.

Stacey sneers.

Meeka and Jolene plant their feet.

Randi squeezes her fists.

Brooke's face burns. "My name isn't *Babs*," she says. "It's *Brooke*. Two *o*'s. No *c*."

Nat snickers. "Whatever you say . . . *Babs*."

Laughter spills from Hawk.

Brooke's eyes flash bright with tears.

She stumbles back.

Slips on the wet grass.

Falls to the ground.

More laughter sifts through the screen.

Brooke scrambles to her feet and bolts to Chickadee.

Nat does a fake gasp. "Oh dear," she says, putting a hand to her lips. "Babs seems upset."

Emillie snaps her gum. "Was it something we said?"

I glare at them, my hands clenched. Brooke Morgan can be mean and bossy and the worst kind of friend sometimes. But, right now, she needs us. And that makes her our extra-best friend.

"It's true," I say.

Emillie tilts her head and looks at me. "What's true?"

"There really is a Meadowlark Monster," I reply.

Then I glance at Nat. *"Two,* actually. I'm looking at them right now."

Nat glares at me.

Emillie sneers.

Liz steps up and takes my hand. "Figaro," she sings.

Emillie shifts her eyes to Liz. "Huh?"

"Figaro," Liz sings again, louder. "It's opera. Monsters hate it."

Jenna grins. Grabs Liz's other hand. "Figaro!"

Stacey, Randi, Meeka, and Jolene grab hands too. We tip our chins to the bright blue sky. And belt it out like divas.

"Figaro . . . Figaro . . . Figaroooooooo!"

Nat shakes her head when we're done. *"Weirdos,"* she says.

"Freaks," Emillie chimes in.

"Takes one to know one," Randi replies.

Then we sing the song again.

Louder.

All the way back to Chickadee.

We're laughing and chattering like chipmunks when we get inside. But as soon as we see Brooke, we go quiet as sock monkeys.

She's lying on her bottom bunk, sobbing into a

pillow that has no pillowcase. Crumpled, like the clothes that are heaped around her. Empty, like the backpack that's fallen to the floor.

She's crying so hard no sound comes out. Her shoulders shake and the bunk creaks.

"This is bad," Randi whispers.

"The baddest," Stacey adds.

"What should we do?" Jolene asks.

No one has an answer. Not even Jenna. So we just stand there. Shuffling our feet. Glancing around. Letting Brooke cry. Because, sometimes, that's all you can do for a friend.

Then something catches my eye.

A monkey tail dangling from my sleeping bag.

I run over.

Grab George.

Hold him out to Brooke.

She hauls him in.

Then Meeka darts to her bunk and pulls something out from her sleeping bag. A moment later, Brooke's got a pink horse with a rainbow tail in the crook of her arm.

Jolene offers a plaid elephant.

Stacey, a teddy bear.

Randi, a frumpy tiger.

Liz, a floppy-eared dog that looks exactly like old Champ.

Even Jenna goes to her bunk and comes back with a bright green beanbag frog. A note is tied to its leg.

Get me a frog!

Love, Rachel

"I told you not to trust them," Jenna says, setting the frog by Brooke. "If you had just listen—"

"Zip it, Jenna," Randi cuts in. "What's done is done."

Jenna stops talking.

"If L-L-Liz had done her j-j-job," Brooke stammers through her tears, "we wouldn't have gotten c-c-caught. Then we could have found Nat and Emillie and n-n-none of this would have happened!"

Liz's eyes go almost as wide as her glasses. "Don't blame me! I didn't make those losers steal your candy!"

Brooke shoots up from the bunk. Clothes fly. Stuffed animals tumble.

She glares at Liz, her hair matted and her face

streaked with tears. "The only loser here is *you,* Liz*butt!*"

"*Brooke*—!" we all shout. Trust me, our voices don't sound one bit huggy-huggy.

Brooke's eyes dart to each of us, like they're looking for a safe place to land. "If she . . . if we . . . if I . . ."

We all cross our arms and do laser eyes at her.

Brooke's lips start trembling again. Her eyes brighten with fresh tears.

She slumps back down. "I'm s-s-sorry," she says. "Nat and Emillie aren't my friends. You guys are."

We huddle around her.

The camp bell rings.

"Weeding time," Jenna says, checking her watch.

"Alex will be back any second," Meeka adds, giving Brooke a sideways hug.

Randi looks around the room. So do I. Animals and clothes are scattered at our feet. Suitcases left open. Brooms dropped, crisscross-applesauce.

"Bye-bye Silver Paddle," Randi says. "This place is a mess."

"*I'm* a mess," Brooke says, smoothing back her tangled hair.

"So what," I say, slinging an arm around Brooke's shoulders. "I'd rather have messy friends than a clean cabin any day."

Everyone nods.

Brooke gives us a smile. Then she sees the empty backpack that's lying on the floor. She sighs. "All that candy. Gone to waste."

"Not all of it," Liz says, reaching into her hoodie pocket. She pulls out the sucker Brooke gave her last night.

Brooke sniffles. "One sucker, *eight* girls?"

Liz smiles. "One is plenty." She unwraps the sucker and takes a lick. "Mmm . . . blue. My favorite flavor."

She offers the sucker to Brooke.

Brooke sniffles again. "You're joking, right?"

Liz shakes her head. "I never joke about blue suckers."

Brooke hesitates. But then she takes the sucker and licks it too.

Then Stacey.

Then Randi.

Then Meeka and Jolene.

Then me.

I hold it out to Jenna.

She wrinkles her nose. "This is totally unsanitary."

"You don't have to do it if you don't want to," I reply.

"Right," Randi says, nodding. "Voluntary licking."

Jenna studies the sucker. Looks at all of us.

Then she takes it.

Squeezes her eyes shut.

And sticks it in her mouth.

We applaud.

And pass the sucker around again.

And again.

And again.

Until we all have matching blue smiles.

The door creaks open. Alex steps in.

Liz snatches the sucker, wraps it up, and tucks it back in her pocket.

We hide our lips.

"Ready for weeding?" Alex asks.

"Mmm-hmm," we all reply.

No one is in a hurry to get to the garden. We're not big fans of weeding. Alex already went ahead to the crafts cottage. Pete is going to supervise our work.

"Hey, Chickadees! Wait up!" someone shouts from behind us as we head down the path past the girls' cabins.

We look back.

Nat and Emillie wave.

We keep walking.

"Give us a chance to explain," Nat says, falling into step with us a moment later. "We were just joking around earlier."

"That's right," Emillie says, draping her long, tan arm around Brooke's shoulders like they're old pals. "We still have your candy. In fact, if you have *more,* we could meet up tonight and have a *real* party!"

Nat nods excitedly. "That would be a total blast!" She twirls a curl and gives us her sweetest smile. "Do you? Have more candy?"

Brooke squirms out from under Emillie's arm. She plants her purple sandals and punches her fists into her hips. "If we *did* have more, we wouldn't share it with *you.*"

Emillie makes her face go all shocked. "But Babs, I thought we were *friends.*"

Brooke crosses her arms. "So did *I*."

Liz nudges in. "Wait, Brooke. Don't be such a meanie. We *did* save some candy . . . remember?"

Liz reaches into her pocket and pulls out the blue sucker.

Our eyes go wide. We suck in our lips.

Brooke studies the sucker for a moment. Then she makes her face go very smooth and flicks back her messy hair.

"Silly me," she says, turning to Nat and Emillie. "I forgot. Liz saved some. Help yourself."

Liz holds the sucker out to Emillie.

Emillie eyes it suspiciously.

We all wait anxiously.

Then, just when I'm sure she won't fall for it, Emillie takes the sucker.

"That's more like it," she says, tossing the wrapper aside. She pops the sucker into her mouth and rolls it around with her tongue. "Mmm, I *love* this flavor."

I nod. "Us too."

Nat budges in. "Hey, what about me?" She eyes Liz's hoodie. "I'm your friend, aren't I?"

Liz pats her empty pockets. "I'm *soooo* sorry,

Nat," she says. "That was the last sucker we *licked*."

Nat blinks.

So does Emillie. She yanks the sucker out of her mouth. "You *didn't*," she says.

Liz smiles.

And sticks out her blue tongue.

We all do.

Emillie throws the sucker onto the path and pokes Liz in the chest. "You little *toad*."

I step up and plant my sneakers next to Liz's cowboy boots. "That's *tadpole* to you."

Randi snorts a laugh.

So do the others.

Emillie storms down the path.

Nat scurries after her.

But they can't get in our way.

We fly right past them.

Sometimes friendship gives you wings.

Chapter

17

Weeding isn't as bad as we thought it would be. We get to wear gardening gloves and, for a boy, Pete has lots of good colors. Pink. Purple. Orange. Blue. Green. Plus, every time a creepy bug crawls anywhere near us, Pete flicks it away before we hardly have time to scream our heads off.

We sing the Camp Meadowlark theme song while we work. And when Rusty, Joey, Quinn, and Tom walk by on their way back from playing kickball, and plug their ears like our singing is poison to their brains, and razz us about getting into trouble, Pete pretends not to notice when we pitch a few rotten tomatoes at them.

"You throw like a girl!" Rusty sings like an opera star, dodging tomatoes.

"Your faces make me hurl!" Joey chimes in.

"Missed me by a mile," Tom adds, snickering.

"Couldn't hit a crocodile!" Quinn bellows, dancing.

"We should sic the Meadowlark Monster on them," Randi grumbles as the boys gallop away, laughing and singing.

"Definitely," Stacey agrees.

"We'd have to lure him in," Meeka offers.

"With what?" Brooke asks. "Rat and Enemmie took all the candy."

"That kind of monster eats campers, not candy," Jolene says.

"Don't ask *me* to volunteer," Randi puts in. "I'm not gonna be monster bait."

"We don't need volunteers," I say. "We don't even need a real monster."

Everyone looks at me.

Stacey's eyes go all curious. "What do you mean?"

I pause, thinking. Then my mouth curls into a sneaky grin.

"I have a plan," I say.

"*You?*" Brooke says back.

"Yes," I reply. "Me. Ida May. And it's a good one."

Liz scoots in. "Spill it."

Everyone else huddles up too.

"We'll need some supplies—" I start to say.

"Wait," Jenna interrupts. She yanks off her gardening gloves and pulls a scrap of paper and a stubby pencil from her jeans pocket. "Okay, go."

"A rope . . ." I say.

Jenna starts writing.

"A bucket of *slime* . . ."

Randi's eyes brighten.

"And . . ." I look across the garden to where Pete is picking beans. "The help of a friend."

Everyone turns and looks at Pete too.

A moment later, he glances up.

"Will you?" I call to him. "Help us trick the boys?"

Pete sits back on his heels.

Wiggles his caterpillar eyebrows.

"At your service, Chickadees."

It turns out you don't need a rope to be a fake monster.

But you do need two clothespins. And eight imaginative friends.

Randi makes the slime on Thursday afternoon. Cornstarch. Water. Green food coloring. Glitter. She tells Alex about our plan and mixes it up in the crafts cottage.

Stacey goes with her and paints one spooky glow-in-the-dark eye on Liz's frog face mask.

Meanwhile, Meeka and Jolene weave a crown out of sticks and weeds and Brooke's purple pageant sash. We decided our monster should be a girl with royal blood.

Pete lets me and Liz borrow a big brown blanket from the lost-and-found box. It looks like it got lost a long time ago, probably in a grave. It smells like the boys after kickball.

We trample the blanket with grass and leaves.

Brooke helps by supervising and thinking up a name for our plan. *The Super-Cool Ultra Monster Mash.* "S-C-U-M-M *scum* for short!" she tells us. "In honor of the boys." She laughs at her own funniness. As usual.

Jenna makes a schedule.

"I'm sleeping in the woods tonight, George," I say, rolling up my sleeping bag as George watches from my bare pillow. "Do you want to come along, or stay here with the others?"

George looks longingly at Brooke's bottom bunk. She donated it to all our stuffed animals so they could have a campout too.

Meeka's rainbow horse.

Jolene's plaid elephant.

Stacey's teddy bear.

Randi's frumpy tiger.

Liz's floppy-eared dog.

We made them sleeping bags out of our pillowcases. And a fake campfire out of rocks and twigs and orange tissue paper. We even saved the mini marshmallows from the trail mix we had for our afternoon snack so they could pretend to toast them.

Jenna had a fit when we brought the marshmallows into the cabin. But Alex looked the other way.

I carry George over to the bunk and set him in his circle of friends.

Then I turn to Liz. She's stuffing her frog face mask and flippers into Brooke's empty backpack to give to Pete. He's bringing the rest of our costume too.

"Front or butt?" I ask her, looking at the face mask and flippers.

She glances up. "Huh?"

"Do you want to be the front end of the monster," I explain, "or do you want to be the back end?" We all voted on who should be the monster. Me and Liz won, 8–0.

Liz thinks for a moment. Then she does that sly grin. "You be the front," she replies. "I'll be the Liz*butt*."

We do a giggle duet.

"Oh my, look at the time," Brooke says, later, Thursday night, at our campsite in the woods. We're toasting marshmallows over the fire Alex and Connor built halfway between the girls' tents and the boys'. "Chop, chop! Time for our night hike. Remember, ladies first, *then* you boys. And *no* flashlights or we won't be able to see the lovely stars."

Brooke doesn't really care about stars, unless she gets to be one on stage. But that's the secret signal we decided to use when it was time to put our SCUMM plan into action.

"I've only had five marshmallows so far," Joey says, leaning back against a log, patting his stomach. "I'm usually good for ten."

"And what about s'mores?" Quinn adds. "I can eat three of those, easy."

"Yeah, Brooke, why the rush?" Rusty asks, licking his sticky fingers. "Can't wait for the Meadowlark Monster to get you?" He gives her a spooky grin.

Brooke gives Rusty an *I-know-something-you-don't-know* smirk. "No monster is going to get *me*."

Pete stands up and stretches. Alex and Connor invited him to stay for supper and s'mores. "I'll get you guys more firewood," he offers. "I could use some help. Any volunteers?"

Right away, me and Liz raise our hands. Not because we're big fans of hauling firewood. But this is part of our plan too.

Pete gives us a wink, then turns to Alex. "We'll catch up with you on the hike," he says.

"At the trust fall platform . . . right?" Alex asks.

"Right," Pete replies.

"Got it," Connor puts in.

They do a three-way smile.

Me and Liz take off with Pete.

Our costume is sitting on the trust fall platform when we get there a few minutes later.

I put on the face mask and pull up the black hood on my extra-large sweatshirt. Randi let me borrow it, compliments of her brother. I snug the hood around my face so mostly just my spooky glowing eye is showing.

Pete smudges a little dirt on my cheeks. Then he dips Liz's green flippers into the slime bucket and slips them on my hands.

I accidentally on purpose flick some slime at Liz.

She squeals and dodges behind me, leaning forward while Pete drapes the big brown blanket over her and around my shoulders so that only our feet are showing. He uses a couple of clothespins to snug the blanket under my chin.

Then he sets the weedy crown on my head.

"Let's hear what you've got," he says, stepping back.

Me and Liz howl like we're the queen of the jungle.

Pete unplugs his ears. "That will do," he says.

Then he slimes my flippers again and ducks into the shadows.

"What's it like back there?" I ask Liz a minute later while we wait for the others to find us.

"Sweaty," comes her muffled reply. "Stinky too. Next Halloween, let's not be the Meadowlark Monster."

I smile to myself, realizing Liz will be around for holidays now.

For regular days too.

Swimming with us at the pool.

Biking to the Purdee Good Café for giant cookies.

Climbing on our new playground equipment.

Acting goofy.

Spilling secrets.

Who knows? I might even tell her I'm going to start liking Quinn again, as soon as he takes a bath. I might tell all my friends.

Voices trickle through the trees.

"They're coming," I say. "Ready?"

"For anything," Liz says back.

"This way!" I hear Jenna shout. "Follow me!"

"Yessss, sir!" Randi shouts back.

Feet trample.

Sticks snap.

Leaves rustle.

Branches shake.

A moment later, Jenna leads everyone into the clearing.

Me and Liz shuffle out from the shadows.

Brooke points at us and does a fake gasp. "What *is* that? It looks like—oh no!—the Meadowlark Monster!" She screams so loud I swear the trees shake. Brooke Morgan is a very good actress.

Me and Liz stamp our feet. Flick slime. Pump out our best howls ever.

All the girls fake freak out.

All the boys freak out for real.

They duck behind Connor. *"Mommy!"* Joey cries.

But Tom peeks out. Gives us the once-over. Switches on a smile.

A moment later, he tips back his chin and starts singing to the starry sky.

"Figaro . . . Figaro . . . Figarooooo!"

Connor joins in.

Then Alex.

Then all the girls.

Then all the boys.

It sounds like the worst opera ever. Or the best, depending on how you look at it.

Flash!

"Got it!" Meeka cries, looking up from her camera. "A picture of the Meadowlark Monster!"

"That's our cue," I whisper to Liz.

"I'm right behind you," she whispers back.

We stomp in a clumsy circle around the trust fall platform, howl once more for show, and then disappear into the woods.

"Take *that,* monster!" Joey cries.

Everyone cheers.

Pete bundles up our costume and hides it under a bush. Then we sneak to the path and slip in behind the others.

"What did we miss?" Pete asks, turning on his flashlight.

"Nothing much," Rusty brags. "We just saved the girls from the Meadowlark Monster, that's all."

Brooke shoots laser eyes at Rusty. "You didn't save us from anything, *Crusty* Smith. *Us* girls can take care of ourselves."

"Yeah," Stacey says, squaring shoulders with Brooke. "Girls rule. Boys drool!"

"*I'm* drooling," Quinn says. "For s'mores." He tilts his head and lets spit dribble from the corner of his mouth.

So gross. Seriously, I need to rethink this crush thing.

"Betchya *girls* can't beat us back!" Joey shouts. He and the other boys take off for the campsite. Connor tags after them.

"Look!" Meeka says, showing us the glowing screen on her camera. "The monster!"

We all huddle in, looking at the picture of me and Liz.

Jenna huffs. "Since when do *monsters* wear cowboy boots?"

Liz grins. "She must be from out west."

Stacey does a puzzled frown and points at the screen. "What's *that*?"

We all look closer at a shadowy shape, off to one side.

"It looks big," Jolene says.

"And furry," Randi adds.

"Like a bear," I say.

"With *one* glowing eye," Liz puts in.

We all do a gasp.

"Ohmy*gosh*!" Brooke says. "It's the *real* Meadowlark Monster!"

"And we got his picture!" Meeka cries, clutching her camera. "Now we'll be famous for sure!"

Everyone starts chattering like chipmunks.

I give Pete a suspicious squint.

He shrugs, all innocent. "I better get that firewood now."

Pete takes off down the path.

"That's enough monsters for tonight," Alex says. "Let's head back before the boys eat all the s'mores."

She starts shooing us toward the path.

But I stop. "Wait," I say. "There's something I want to do first."

I hurry to the trust fall platform and scramble up. "I haven't fallen yet," I say. "Catch me, okay?"

"In the dark?" Jenna says. "That's totally unsafe."

"We've got light," Alex says, pulling a flashlight from her pocket. She shines its bright beam down the girls' arms as they line up below me.

"All systems go!" Randi says. "Ten . . . nine . . . eight . . ."

Everyone joins in.

I turn around as they count down, and reach my hands up to the star-speckled sky. I'm not even standing on my tiptoes, but I swear I can touch it.

Then I straighten my back.

Cross my arms.

Lock my knees.

Take a brave breath.

"Falling!" I shout.

"Fall away!" everyone shouts back.

So I do.

Just like a domino.

My friends don't let me down.

Chapter

18

Brooke was right about one thing this week. She never did go off the trust fall platform.

But I still think she fell.

And we caught her.

Me, Stacey, Jenna, Liz, Randi, Meeka, and Jolene.

Not in our arms.

In our friendship.

She also isn't going to dance at our talent show today. Even though her mom brought a bouquet of flowers to give her afterward. It's Friday afternoon and all of our families are arriving to watch the show and then take us home. Even Liz's dog, Champ, is here with her family. Cee Cee too, with her arm in a sling.

"It isn't a competition, Mother!" Brooke tells

Mrs. Morgan when she sees the bouquet of flowers. "It's just for *fun*. With my *friends*." Brooke crosses her arms against the crumpled purple sash she's wearing over her Camp Meadowlark T-shirt. She's also wearing her pageant crown. And buggy sunglasses. And Liz's flippers on her feet. When it's our cabin's turn to do a skit, Brooke is going to waddle across the stage, waving like she's queen of the beach.

Then the rest of us will join her in *our* Camp Meadowlark T-shirts and chant, "Hot or cool! Chickadees *rule!*" Get it? Plus, we're going to hand out glow-in-the-dark ladybugs to everyone in the audience. Even Rat and Enemmie.

I'm looking around for my mom and dad, but I see the boys first. They're showing off the Silver Paddle they won for having the cleanest cabin.

We were in total shock and awe when Connor presented it to them at breakfast this morning. But I guess it makes sense that they won. There were only four campers in their group. Plus, they wore the same stinky clothes all week. It's hard to mess up a cabin if you never open your suitcase.

After Connor gave them the paddle and took their picture and did a group head-lock, he said, "I'm gonna miss you monkeys." Joey Carpenter actually had tears in his eyes, and I don't think it was from the knuckle rub.

I'm not crying, though. None of my friends are. Because we don't have to miss each other for long. We're all meeting at the Purdee pool tomorrow for Brooke's *Post-Camp Splash Bash!* Jenna's working on the schedule. Meeka will take pictures so we can send some to Alex. Everyone is bringing snacks. *Tons.* Including blue suckers.

"Did you have a fun week?" Mom asks when she and Dad finally arrive.

"Yes," I reply, hugging them hello.

"Pull any pranks?" Dad asks, tousling my hair. I hate when he does that, but today I don't mind because, trust me, my hair is already tossed.

I give Jenna and Liz a sly glance.

They give me two back.

"Just one," I tell Dad.

He grins. "Details?"

But we shake our heads. There are some things your parents just don't need to know about.

"Jen!"

Rachel pushes through the tangle of people and hugs her sister hard. "Did you miss me?" she asks.

"Duh," Jenna replies, hugging Rachel back.

Rachel looks up hopefully. "Where's my frog?"

Jenna rolls her eyes. "No frog, Rachel. I told you that a million times. You should have believed me."

Rachel sighs. "I *did* believe you," she grumps. "But I hoped I was wrong."

"I have a frog," Liz says.

Rachel brightens. "You do?"

Jenna squints. "You do not."

Liz dashes to our pile of suitcases and sleeping bags. She finds her beach bag and pulls out her frog face mask. Most of the glow-in-the-dark paint is rubbed off.

"For you," she says, holding it out to Rachel.

Rachel's eyes go wide. She takes the mask from Liz. "For me?"

Liz nods. "For keeps!"

She glances at me. We do matching smiles.

"Ribbit! Ribbit! Ribbit!" Rachel croaks, over

and over and over again as she hops in a circle around Jenna.

Jenna crosses her arms and gives Liz a look. "Thank you *soooo* much, Liz Evans," she says.

Liz grins back. "You're *soooo* welcome, Jenna Drews."

"Ida! Liz! Jenna! Over here!"

We look toward the beach and see Randi waving. Meeka is lining up the other girls. Brooke is tossing aside her beach queen stuff and smoothing back her hair. "Hurry! Group shot!"

Rachel hops over to her parents.

We join the other girls. Even the boys bunch in, pumping the Silver Paddle over their heads.

"Say *cheese*!" Meeka cries, holding up her camera.

"Cheese!" all us girls sing.

"Cheese *turds*!" the boys chime in.

We do a few poses. Serious. Silly. Glamour.

Click! . . . Click! . . . Click!

"Let me take one, Meeka," Liz offers, stepping out of the shot. "Or you won't be in any of the pictures!"

Meeka gives her camera to Liz.

Liz takes aim.

"No, no, let *me* do that."

Mrs. Morgan walks up to Liz and takes the camera. Then she looks over at Brooke and gives her a smile.

Mrs. Morgan hands her bouquet of flowers to Liz. "Welcome home, dear," she says.

Liz's eyes go wide behind her glasses. "Thank you!" she says, smelling the bouquet.

"Now shoo," Mrs. Morgan says, waving Liz away. "Stand with your friends."

Liz clomps back to us.

We haul her in.